PARIS FEVER

Recovering from a broken engagement, Jenny is sent to Paris to research her father's novel. Jenny wanted to be independent but her father insisted that David, an old friend, would look after her. When she finally met the charismatic American, she knew that her sixth sense had been right.

JANE GURNEY

PARIS FEVER

Complete and Unabridged

LINFORD
Leicester

First published in Great Britain in 1986 by
IPC Magazines Limited
London

First Linford Edition
published June 1991

Copyright © 1986 by Jane Gurney
All rights reserved

British Library CIP Data

Gurney, Jane
Paris fever.—Large print ed.—
Linford romance library
I. Title
823.914 [F]

ISBN 0–7089–7050–8

Published by
F. A. Thorpe (Publishing) Ltd.
Anstey, Leicestershire

Set by Words & Graphics Ltd.
Anstey, Leicestershire
Printed and bound in Great Britain by
T. J. Press (Padstow) Ltd., Padstow, Cornwall

1

WHEN the phone rang, Jenny Chatham was halfway up a stepladder, engaged in painting the walls of her sitting-room a sombre midnight blue. She balanced the brush across the top of the can and snatched up the receiver.

"Ashfield 37961. Oh, hello, Dad."

"I got your note," said the distant voice. "I'm really sorry, Jenny. Are you very upset about it?"

"No," she said. "Piers was quite right. It wouldn't have worked, and it's better to find that out now than later, even if it does mean sending back the toasters and the crystal. Oh, thanks for your present, by the way. I'll bring it back to you some time if I may. The postage would be too enormous."

"No need to bother about that." Her father sounded embarrassed. "The main thing is, are you all right?"

"I'm always all right."

"How does it affect your job?"

"Basically, I'm unemployed right now," Jenny said, matter-of-factly. "It would have been a bit awkward, carrying on as Piers' assistant in the circumstances. He did offer to let me stay on, of course."

"Have you anything else in mind?"

"Not yet. I'm taking some time off to redecorate my flat, then I'll look around for something"

"Are you OK for money?"

"Yes thanks, Dad." It was true for the time being, but she was a bit worried about her long-term prospects. Not that she was about to tell her father that. She had gone straight from school to university, and thereafter to Piers Somerton, Fine Art Auctioneers, initially as his clerical assistant.

It was a lowly position, but the chance to learn about antiques fascinated her. She had hoped one day to have a shop of her own but becoming Piers' girl friend, and later his fiancée, had distracted her from her business ambitions, although getting married had proved to be an infinitely postponable event. They had finally got round to sending out invitations and notices to *The Times* after two and a half years... at which point Piers had suddenly developed cold feet and expressed his qualms about the finality of matrimony.

It had been a reflection of Jenny's own doubts, and she had handed back his ring with something like relief. All the same, it was hard to readjust to a life without the certainty of Piers' affection in it, and jobs in the antique trade were not going to be easy to come by. Nor would her capital stretch to finding premises of her own. Her English degree in itself didn't equip her for much else in the employment field.

"I have a few possibilities lined up for consideration," Jenny lied to her father on the phone.

"That's good. But nothing immediate?"

"No," she admitted.

"Then I have a proposition that might

interest you. You've never been to Paris, have you?"

"No," she said again.

"I was there for several months last year, researching background for my latest novel. There are flashbacks to the revolution, because the main character gets involved with a family who have a sort of historical skeleton in their cupboard.

"The trouble is, now I'm getting down to writing it, I find that there are certain odd details I missed. Scenes set in the *Conciergerie*, for instance, where I can't for the life of me remember which side of the window the door is in a particular room, or the colour of the curtains in one of the *salons* at Versailles.

"I could just flannel about things like that, but I find you always get rude letters from your readers, picking out the inaccurate details. Also, I find it hard to put myself in the position of a young girl, like my heroine in the twentieth century part of the story, who is seeing Paris for the first time. I've been there so often, I've forgotten what that first glimpse was like. I did mean to go over for a few days just to fill in some of the gaps, but I've been invited by the BBC to do a chat show about the launch of the last book, and I find I can't fit it in. Rather than cancel the plane ticket, I thought you might like to use it, and do my research for me as well."

"But I'm not experienced at that sort of thing," Jenny demurred.

"There's no need to be. All you'd have to do is visit various places — I'd prepare a list — and note the outstanding details. And jot down some impressions of the city. I'd pay all your expenses, and a small fee, and you could have a bit of a holiday as well."

It was a tempting prospect, a lot more fun than slapping midnight blue on to the walls. She had selected the colour on impulse, to match her gloomy mood, and was already beginning to feel it had been a mistake.

"Well . . ." Jenny considered. "It

sounds like a very pleasant idea. When would you want me to go?"

"The outward ticket is from Gatwick," her father said, "leaving at twelve fifty-four this morning. But they do like you to check in about forty minutes earlier."

"But that would be twelve o'clock this morning! Less than three hours. It would take me at least an hour to drive to Gatwick."

"Can't you manage that?" he asked. Her globe-trotting father was used to setting off anywhere at a moment's notice. "How about your passport? Is that in order?"

"Oh, that's OK. I have one of those British Visitor things still valid from my last Spanish holiday with Piers. But there are clothes to pack, and people to phone. And what about a hotel?"

"No problem," he said airily. "Just sling a few basics in a suitcase. Then, when you get there, buy anything you find you need in Paris. Go on a spree. I'll arrange for some money to be transferred to my bank's Paris branch, in the Place Vendôme."

"There's no need for that, Dad."

"I'd like to give you some clothes," he insisted. "It's something you've missed out on in the past, and now my books are selling so well, I'd enjoy seeing you in some Paris finery. I am your father, after all."

"So you are," Jenny said ironically. "I keep forgetting."

There was a momentary silence at the other end of the phone. She supposed she had hurt his feelings. But he had walked out of her life when he divorced her mother, and she still felt reluctant to let him take over the rôle of parent again, in spite of his generosity.

"As for hotels," his voice said, carefully glossing over the sour note she had introduced, "an old friend of mine is in Paris right now, on a working holiday. I was going to stay with him. You might find that arrangement a bit awkward, but I'll ring him and explain what's happening and he can fix you up. He knows his way about. I'll get him to meet you at the airport."

"But if he's working, surely he won't want to spare the time?"

"Oh, David won't mind. He's a good friend. He'd do anything for me," her father said expansively. "You've got a lot in common. He sells antiques, too. Eighteenth-century furniture is his main interest, but he does all sorts. He has another lucrative sideline as well . . . He's American, by the way. You'll like him. Most women seem to."

'But I'm not 'most women',' Jenny thought rebelliously, already picturing some smooth-tongued, silver-haired charmer. "There's no need to ring this man," she said. "I can manage perfectly well by myself. When would I come back?"

"Next Sunday. Then you've agreed to go?"

"Yes, I'll go. And thanks."

"Marvellous. Then my secretary will meet you at the Air France check-in at Gatwick with the tickets and the research list at around eleven forty-five. I wish I could come and see you off myself, but I'm up to my eyes — "

"That's OK, Dad. You don't have to bother about that."

"See you when you get back, then. Enjoy Paris."

She put down the receiver and tried to organise her thoughts. It was just after nine-fifteen. Clothes, cancel milk and papers, dash down to the bank's foreign till for currency. Passport. Ring mother. An hour's drive to Gatwick. And all by eleven forty-five!

She made it, with minutes to spare, but still dressed in her old painting jeans, an outsize shirt that had belonged to Piers, and no make-up. Her hair was a mess, rapidly escaping from her knot in which she had pinned it to keep it out of paint's way. Her anorak had seen better days, and her shoes were spotted with splashes of midnight blue. She had hastily tipped an armful of the contents of her wardrobe into a suitcase, and was still trying to work out what she might have forgotten when she collected an envelope from her father's latest secretary, a sophisticated blonde with a porcelain complexion who made her feel totally inadequate.

Ruffled, she made her way to the departure lounge. The plane was delayed. A problem, it seemed, with undercarriage checks. In the next two hours, Jenny bought and read a magazine, watched her fellow passengers fretting, splurged more than she should on a bottle of *Arpège* from the duty-free perfume counter, did the magazine's cross word, and read the articles all over again.

At last the plane took off, and less than an hour after that she landed, simmering with impatience, at L'Aéroport Charles de Gaulle.

There was the usual jockeying for position in the queue for customs, which she bore with scant patience, and at last she emerged to see a man in uniform holding up a piece of card printed with her name. He seemed to be an airline employee.

"Miss Chatham? I 'ave a message for you."

He handed her a sheet of paper which, when unfolded, revealed a message written in a forward-slanting, decisive hand.

"*Couldn't wait any longer,*" it said, tersely. "*Back as soon as I can manage. Please wait in café by Gate 37. David Maine.*" The signature was assertively underlined, twice.

So her father had rung the man after all. What a nuisance! Judging by the tone of his note, the unknown Mr. Maine wasn't any too pleased to be dragged away from his business affairs to meet her, either.

She sat down reluctantly at one of the formica tables in the cafeteria, and ordered coffee and a sandwich.

Another hour crawled by. The cafeteria was brightly lit and noisy, and she was constantly bumped and jostled by people coming and going to the counter. She ordered another coffee and watched it grow cold, her impatience mounting to screaming point. Beyond the automatic glass doors, coaches to Paris were leaving at twenty-minute intervals, yet here she sat, waiting for this Maine character, who might or might not reappear this side of midnight.

She had asked the waiter at the bar, in hesitant French, if anyone had come looking for an English girl. No, he replied. Not that he knew of. No one had asked him. At least it was a relief to find that if she spoke slowly, and he replied slowly, she could make herself understood. She tried, asking for the whereabouts of the nearest ladies' cloakroom, and adding that she would be gone for several minutes. If the man came to look for her, could he be asked to wait?

"*Oue, Mademoiselle, je lui dirai que vous allez retourner.*"

She went in search of the ladies' room, on another floor; it took a while to find it, and there was a problem with the lift which didn't seem to respond to the buttons she pressed. Nothing was going right today. "I wish I'd stayed at home," she muttered under her breath. When she found another lift, and reached the cloakroom at last, her reflection in the mirror was not inspiring.

She had clear, creamy skin, wide green eyes and thick auburn hair that owed nothing to dye for the depth of its colour, but in her painting gear she looked like Orphan Annie. The faded jeans were fraying at the hem, her anorak was crumpled and there was a smudge of blue paint on her jaw which couldn't be scrubbed off with mere water. The paint spots on her hair she could do nothing about either. She grimaced despairingly at herself in the mirror and gave it up as a bad job.

When she got back to the cafeteria, the waiter rushed up to her excitedly.

"*Mademoiselle! Vôtre monsieur, l' Américain, il est arrivé. Mais attention! Il s'en va!* 'E is going!"

She caught a glimpse of a man's back, dressed in an immaculate charcoal grey suit, disappearing round the corner of one of the display cases in the open corridor beyond the café.

"Hey!" She ran after him, dragging her case and shoulder bag. "Are you looking for me? I'm Jenny Chatham."

The man stopped and turned.

He was not at all what she had expected. He was one of the most good-looking young men she had ever laid eyes on, off a cinema or television screen. In fact a movie talent scout would probably snap him up like a shot, she thought, for starring rôles in soap operas about oil magnates. From his dark, well-cut hair to his expensive shoes, he was immaculate. The severely tailored, impeccably fitted charcoal suit, and the pale grey shirt clad a slim, athletic figure. His face was lean and clean-shaven, with well-shaped features, a strong, decisive mouth and chin and straight dark eyebrows above deep-set, intensely blue eyes. In the first week of June, he had, unfairly, a tan.

He looked not a day over thirty. He didn't look particularly pleased to see her.

"I told you to wait in the cafeteria," he snapped. "Didn't you get my note? I darn nearly missed you." He had a faint, rather that a marked American accent, and a voice which, had he been saying something pleasant, might have had an attractive timbre. As it was, his curt tone inflamed Jenny's already frayed temper. She dumped her case and shoulder bag on the carpet at his feet and bristled.

"I have been to the ladies' cloakroom," she stated, baldly. "I am only human. I have had a two-hour delay, one-hour flight, and another hour hanging about waiting for you to turn up."

He glared back.

"Well, now that we've finally met up, let's not waste any more time. Are those all your things?" Without bothering to wait for a reply, he scooped them up and headed for the nearest doorway.

"I'm parked where I shouldn't be," he said over his shoulder. "So could we kindly get a move on?"

"Of all the rude, offhand, casual louts," she muttered to herself, inaudibly. Of course, men like him didn't need charm. They got by on sheer good looks and machismo.

She strolled after him, deliberately slowing her pace. "You shouldn't have wasted your valuable time, Mr. Maine," she informed him sweetly. "I really didn't need to be met. I'm quite capable of looking after myself."

"I can well believe it," he retorted. "Pity nobody told George Acre. He rang this morning and told me his assistant would be arriving to do some research, and would I *please* collect you and look after you because you'd never been to Paris. He made you sound so helpless, I was expecting a vague academic with pebble lenses, or a timid schoolgirl. You look perfectly capable of catching the airline bus to me."

"Well, now we've established that, you can get back to your busy life and I can just hop on the bus," Jenny told him.

"No way. After all the trouble I've taken to get back here, I'm driving you into Paris."

"There's no need," she said icily. "In fact, I'd prefer that you didn't."

"I'm just doing what George asked me to do," he said. "And, since you work for him, maybe you should try doing the same."

"Actually, he's not my employer. He's my father."

He stopped in his tracks. "You're George's *daughter*? I thought you looked familiar, somehow. But your name — ?"

"My mother remarried. It's my stepfather's surname — if it's any of your business."

He dumped her bags on to the pavement as she spoke, and cut in curtly, "Wait here. I'll get the car."

He strode rapidly away, and she hovered irritably by the luggage, half-inclined to take it over to the airport bus which was currently being loaded up in one of the farther bays. As she hesitated, his car drew up beside her, a silver grey Lotus Élite with French number plates. 'Typical,' she thought.

He loaded her luggage and minutes later they were edging into the stream of traffic on the motorway. He was clearly used to driving in France, judging by the ease with which he wove his way past slower vehicles. She would have had to concentrate, to adapt to driving on the right hand side of the road. But presumably things were different in America anyway.

Jenny was looking straight ahead of her but she could see his hands, moving between controls and wheel, out of the corner of her eye. They were brown and capable, spare and shapely, with well-kept fingernails. She was acutely aware of his physical perfection, and of her own scruffy appearance.

"Where do you want to go?" he asked. "The Ritz? The Hilton?"

"Oh, no," she said hastily. "Something much less expensive."

"There's no need to worry about the expense. George said I should make sure you have everything you need, show you round, pay the bills and he'd settle with me later. But it's true you don't look the Ritzy type."

Jenny flushed. "I can pay my own bills," she said coldly. "But I don't see the point of squandering money unnecessarily."

He ignored the put-down. "Then what about a family hotel? I know one in Passy which is clean and comfortable, in a quiet square away from traffic. It's just bed and breakfast, but there are plenty of good restaurants about. I stay there myself sometimes."

"That sounds fine," Jenny said. "I gather that you aren't staying there now?" she added.

"No, I have the loan of a flat at present. A flat and this car."

"Oh, so it's not yours?"

"No, just borrowed."

"What a pity," she commented. "It goes so well with your suit."

He shot her a keen, assessing look. "I gather you're still in a filthy temper. I guess it goes with the hair."

"You're not exactly a ray of sunshine

either," Jenny retorted. She thought that she had never met anyone so gratuitously rude on such short acquaintance. Maybe 'most women' liked that sort of thing, as George had implied, but certainly not her.

She turned her face away and watched the open scenery of the motorway merge with the warehouses, tower blocks and factory complexes that made up the outskirts of the city. There was a hostile silence between them as the car wove its way through streets of tall grey stone buildings, past brightly awned shops and signposts painted with names that struck echoes throughout the world: Tour d'Eiffel, Champs-Elysées, Place de la Concorde, Montmartre . . .

At last the Lotus drew up in front of a tall building with long windows overlooking a paved square. There were rowan trees planted round the square, their trunks fenced in by wrought iron palisades. The windows were balconied with railings of the same intricate wrought iron, and boxes on the balconies dripped tassels of pink and red fuchsias. Most of the long windows were open to the light and air, their louvred shutters folded back, and the interiors of the rooms were screened by white gauze curtains which drifted in the breeze.

"Well, this is it," David Main said. "Will it do?"

Jenny forgot her animosity. In the early evening sunlight the square looked very elegant and very French, and yet welcoming, with the sounds of music, and cooking, and conversation coming faintly from the open windows of the various houses. She began to realise that she was in Paris, the city of romance, and to be excited by it. Unconsciously, she smiled at David as she got out of the car.

"It looks lovely," she said.

David raised his eyebrows. "I don't believe it," he said to the heavens at large. "The lady actually smiled."

"Don't worry," Jenny snapped, the smiling fading instantly. "It's not infectious."

"Now, don't get on your high horse," he said. "It was a very nice smile. You should use it more often. You'd better wait here while I check up on vacancies. It's still off-season but this is a popular hotel. We might have to try somewhere else."

He was back a couple of minutes later.

"It's OK, they've got a double room with a shower cubicle. You're lucky — it's a late cancellation. No single rooms left, but they tend to be cramped anyway. Oh, by the way, I forgot to ask. How's your French? They don't speak much English here."

"Adequate, I think."

"That's all right, then." He unloaded her luggage and led her into the cool reception hall, with its floor paved in black and white stone tiles. The receptionist, a severely-coiffed middle-aged lady with a formidable bust, was dressed in starchy black-and-white to match the décor. David's French was rapid, fluent and, to Jenny's ears, indistinguishable in accent from that of the *patronne*. She was again impressed, against her will, by his casual competence.

She was shown to a room on the first floor; light and spacious, prettily curtained and filled with a geranium scent from beyond the open windows overlooking the square. She looked around appreciatively, David deposited her case on a low, slatted stool at the foot of the bed, and glanced at his watch.

"I'll leave you to unpack. I have an appointment," he said. "But I've booked us a table for tonight at *Les Quatre Saisons*, in the Marais. That's the oldest part of Paris. The table is reserved for eight-thirty."

"There's really no need — " she began.

"I know," he interrupted. "So you keep saying. But I've booked it, so you may as well eat." As she hesitated, he added frankly, "Look, I know you were expecting some avuncular old man to show you the sights, m'dear, and complement you on your well-turned ankle. I was expecting a sweet and amenable young thing who'd listen wide-eyed to my tales of the Big City, so we're neither of us what the other one anticipated. And the waiting around was a damned nuisance. But I did promise George to show you round, and maybe things will improve when we're better acquainted. So what do you say?"

"All right."

"I'll call for you at eight o'clock, then." In the doorway, he turned. "Oh, incidentally, this restaurant is fairly ... uh ... formal. Is that all right?" His eyes dwelt meaningfully on her jeans and anorak.

"I do have other clothes. What had you in mind? Floor-length gold lamé with a spattering of diamonds?"

"Just an evening sort of dress."

"I may just be able to manage that," Jenny said with heavy sarcasm.

"Eight o'clock," he said, and left.

2

PARADOXICALLY, because she loathed David Maine, Jenny took a lot of trouble getting ready for the evening. First, having reviewed the contents of her suitcase with some dismay, she decided that the only outfit that qualified as 'formal,' was a three-piece in peridot green, the colour of her eyes. The opaque, silk-lined voile of the skirt swirled from a deep waistband which emphasised her narrow waist and slim hips. The skimpy, low-cut silk camisole top, tied at the shoulders with shoe-string straps, was given decorum by a matching jacket, whose lapels echoed the cut-work embroidery of the camisole.

She arranged for the outfit to be pressed by a helpful chambermaid, and washed her hair, banishing all traces of midnight blue emulsion. When it was dry, she experimented with various styles of pinning it up, hoping for sophstication, but it was too heavy and too slippery in its newly-washed state so she settled for brushing it into a sleek curtain of a long bob, falling to her shoulders. She was applying mascara to her long lashes, under a sweep of green shadow, when the chambermaid brought back the freshly-ironed clothes.

"Mais, Mademoiselle, regardez: la veste manque un bouton."

To her dismay, Jenny saw that the woman was right. One of the tiny, silk-covered buttons of the jacket was missing. She searched through her case, but there was no sign of it. It must be lying on the floor of her wardrobe at home. It was already seven-thirty, and there would be no chance of buying replacement buttons.

She would just have to go without a jacket, although she had never dared to wear the brief camisole top without one before now.

Promptly at eight, there was a knock on the door. David Maine looked elegant in a dinner jacket, like a Sunday supplement advertisement for Moss Bros. His eyebrows lifted slightly when he saw her, but it was his only acknowledgement of her painstaking transformation.

"Are you ready?" he asked.

"Yes, I think so. Is this sufficiently formal?"

"It looks all right," he said non-committally. "But you'll need something warmer over it." His glance flickered over her bare shoulders.

"I don't get cold," Jenny said.

"It might be wise to take a cardigan or something."

"I don't have a cardigan," she said, nettled. "And I'll be quite warm enough without one."

David shrugged, and held open the door for her to pass through. Walking downstairs in front of him, she rather wished after all that she had a shawl, or something, to cover her back and shoulders. They felt very bare and exposed where the back of the camisole scooped low, almost to her waist. Not that her urbane companion would be bothering to look, she reminded herself.

David had a taxi waiting, instead of the silver grey Lotus. "Easier for parking," he informed her. They were driven through a maze of streets towards the oldest part of the city. She watched the kaleidoscope of tall stone buildings, broad open squares, trees and fountains and elegant shops, give way to the shabbier, less spacious, but still beautiful streets of the St. Paul area, almost forgetting the silent man beside her because she was so interested in the scenes through which the taxi was passing. There were people everywhere, strolling along the pavements or sitting companionably at small tables set out under the striped awnings of the many bar-tabacs and restaurants they passed.

Las Quatre Saisons, where David had booked a table, was in a different category. Here, there were no cheerful tables spilling into the street outside, just curtained windows and a discreetly displayed, hand-written menu in a glass case beside the door. Inside, it was shadowy with soft lamp light and candlelight, the tables shining with silver, crystal and pale, immaculate linen. Every table seemed to be occupied by a couple in expensive evening dress: the men in sombre black and white, the ladies glittering with jewels and swathed in silks or floating chiffons, unmistakably haute couture in their origins.

Jenny tried to bolster her confidence with a recall of the frankly appreciative glances she had received from the taxi driver but she felt nervous and gauche. It was ridiculous, she told herself sternly, because she had been to plenty of high quality restaurants with Piers. The difference was then she had been at ease with her escort, able to take the luxurious settings for granted, assured that in Piers' eyes she was in no way fitted to her surroundings. Now, in David Maine's company, she felt as if she had something to prove. The green dress, she thought, passed muster — but only just.

The discreet music wasn't piped — there was a quartet playing in an alcove at the end of the room, and even a small dance floor surrounded by banks of flowering plants.

To her relief, she found that she could understand the menu. David passed their order to a waiter, chose wine with crisp decision from the extensive wine list, and regarded her across the small table.

"I hope you like French food?"

"Yes. What I've had of it so far."

"Is this your first trip to France? I knew you'd never been to Paris."

"No, I spent some time in Bordeaux a few years ago." It had been a school trip in the sixth form, but she was not about to tell him that. It sounded so unsophisticated.

"So you're no stranger to French cuisine."

From what Jenny could recall, the hotel chosen by the school tour organisers had chiefly served up chicken and chips. She wondered whether it was necessary to admit that the refinements of Cordon

Bleu were largely new to her. At that moment a white-jacketed Frenchman — the manager? The head waiter? — came by and stopped to shake hands. "*Ah, Monsieur Maine, bonsoir! Nous sommes enchanté de vous voir encore. J'espère que tout va bien?*" They exchanged pleasantries and he moved on, with a final bow in Jenny's direction. "*Bon appétit, Mademoiselle.*"

"You're clearly no stranger here, anyway," Jenny observed.

"No, I tend to come in several times every trip, and I've been to Paris at least twice a year for the last sixteen years."

"My father said you knew your way around."

David smiled. It was the most friendly look he had given her so far.

"It's George I have to thank for that. The first time I came I was twelve years old. George was sweet on my Mom at the time. I think they were considering getting married. Mom had just gotten her second divorce. I suspect he was anxious to demonstrate his paternal abilities, to clinch the deal so to speak, because he took me all over the city and really gave me a whale of a holiday for two glorious months. I just fell in love with Paris, and I've been back every chance I got since then. Poor George . . . he didn't get his just reward, because the last thing Mom's interested in is paternal abilities. They never did get married but we've stayed in touch. The thing about George — " he said affectionately — "is that he seems off-hand and undemonstrative on the outside, but underneath he's got a real soft centre, only he's scared to let it show."

"I wouldn't know," Jenny said. "I'm only his daughter."

He caught the irony in her comment. "You must think I've got a nerve, I guess, giving you personality rundowns on your father as if he was a stranger to you. You're right, of course."

"No, you're right," Jenny stated baldly. "He *is* a stranger to me. He was in Paris with you sixteen years ago. That was the year he walked out on Mum and me. He just left us, one fine day, and I didn't see him again until this year. Oh, he used to send us money for our maintenance. And birthday presents. He was very good at remembering those, although they were never actually anything I wanted. Well, how would he know? The only reason I'm in touch with him now is that he saw the notice of my engagement in *The Times* and wrote to congratulate me. He suggested we should meet, and I've seen him a few times since then when he's plied me with presents. But you know him infinitely better than I do."

Listening to David's account of his friendship with her father she had felt a surge of jealousy. She was remembering very clearly the year when she was eight years old, and her mother had seemed to be endlessly crying or else terrifyingly apt to fly into a rage if the small Jenny dared to ask her why Daddy had gone away. In their meetings this year, George had implied that Jenny's mother had refused to let him have access to her after the divorce as a form of retribution. He had thought it wiser to stay away than to have constant upset and bitterness intruding into her life, he explained.

David looked embarrassed. "I'm sorry," he said ruefully. "I didn't realise . . . He never said . . . Oh, I knew about the divorce from your Mom, of course, but I just assumed he'd gone on seeing you. He always seemed to know about you, how your schooling was going and so on. I remember how pleased he was when you got to university. And there were photos of you about although, now I come to think about it, I've never seen anything more recent than that schoolgirl one with the plaits. I guess they must have been hard to come by. But I do know he cares a lot about you."

"He's had a funny way of showing it."

"Don't be too hard on him," David said quietly. "Divorce can be a hell of a mess. I know: my Mom went through it quite a few times — though in the end she got it down to a fine art through sheer practice!" he added lightheartedly, deliberately introducing a less serious note to the conversation. Jenny smiled back at him reluctantly. He certainly had charm, when he wanted it. It was difficult to stay resentful in the face of that quizzical look which invited her to join in with the joke. And, after all, it wasn't his fault that George had preferred another woman's child to his own.

"So. Your Mom married again?" he said, after a moment.

"Yes. How did you know that?"

"You told me this afternoon, at the airport."

"Did I? Oh, yes." At the time he had been so brusque, she had not expected him to notice anything she said.

"So how did you get on with your stepfather?"

"He was all right," she said slowly, recalling the polite, distant relationship she had had with the man her mother had married when she was thirteen. "He and Mum had two more children together, and obviously he felt closer to them. But he was quite kind."

David watched her keenly. "Poor kid," he said quietly.

She flushed, finding his sympathy hard to take. "I said he was all right," she said sharply. "I'm not retailing any wicked stepfather stories. You don't have to feel sorry for me."

His look changed, became harder. "OK, Miss Independent," he said, shrugging his shoulders. "Let's talk about something else. Hasn't it been a lovely day? The English always discuss the weather first, don't they? Now it's your turn."

The arrival of the first course interrupted the conversation at that point. They made polite, stilted small talk at intervals throughout the meal. While they waited for coffee, Jenny recalled her father's comment that she and David had a job with antiques in common. She realised that they had hardly talked about David at all over dinner. It had been merely his questions and her monosyllabic answers, most of the time.

"My father said you were working in antiques. Is that why you are in Paris?" she asked.

"Partly, yes, though I have another sideline which I'm also working on at the moment. But I have some clients over here who like English style antiques, and customers in England who prefer the French style, so I drive a van over stuffed with Regency and Early Victorian furniture — the locals seem to like the very plain lines — and take it back full of Empire Day beds and chandeliers, when I can get them. It works out pretty well, usually, though the paperwork from this end can be complicated. Anyway, it pays for the trip."

"But I thought you lived in America?" Jenny asked.

"Not any more. Not for a long time, as a matter of fact. Mom got married to an Englishman last time round, having worked her way through a selection of Europeans, and this time it's lasting surprisingly well. I've lived in so many places I was feeling pretty stateless by then, and England suits me as well as anywhere else so I set up business there, in Henley on Thames. It's a good trading position, and the countryside is pretty. What is it you do?"

"I'm an auctioneer's assistant," Jenny said. "Or I was, until a couple of weeks ago."

"Did you get fired?"

"No. I left."

"Which auctioneer was it?"

"Somerton's, of Ashfield in Kent."

"I've heard of them. They're a successful firm, aren't they? Good quality stuff for a provincial auctions rooms. Why did you leave?"

"For personal reasons," Jenny said, reluctant to launch into details. David was an odd mixture. He had been so off-hand at first, even downright unfriendly. Then this evening he seemed to be finding out quite a lot about her in this casual way, and she was uncomfortable about the amount she had been giving away.

He had just asked her something. She

came out of her reverie. "Sorry, what did you say?"

"I said, do you dance?"

He seemed to take the answer for granted because he was already standing, ready to move her chair back for her. She let him lead her to the dance floor, with his hand lightly under her elbow, but suddenly her heart was pounding and she found that she didn't welcome the prospect of such close proximity. She was furious with herself. She wasn't a shrinking schoolgirl any more, so why on earth should she be reduced to a state of near panic by the idea of spending a few short minutes in the arms of a man? Even though the man in question was unfamiliar, unpredictable, and the most physically stunning male she had ever met!

There were plenty of other couples on the dance floor, and it was more dimly lit than the dining area, for which she was grateful, aware that her cheeks were hot. Luckily the four-piece band had settled into playing slow, smoky music suitable for romantic shuffling, so she wasn't going to be called upon to show off her unpractised disco dancing style . . . but she wasn't sure if romantic shuffling might not be worse from the point of view of nerves. David put his hands lightly on either side of her waist and they moved around decorously for about fifteen awkward seconds, then he said casually, "I rather think the prevailing style is cheek to cheek. Do you mind?"

"No," said Jenny untruthfully, blushing furiously.

He shifted his hands and brought her closer. She put her arms up and around his neck, acutely conscious of the slight pressure of his hard, supple figure along the length of her body. Her heartbeat might almost have been audible, it was so rapid. His clean-shaven cheek and jaw rested gently against the side of her forehead, his hands held her firmly, the fingers spread across her back above and below the low-cut silk of the top. She was aware of the different sensations of his hands, the still sleeves of his jacket, and the cold metal of his watchband against her bare skin. The scent of him, clean and warm, faintly tinged with aftershave lotion, and the wine they had drunk mixed with her own perfume, making her feel breathless and slightly dizzy. She followed his movements a little hesitantly, too tense to let her body relax against him. When the music stopped, she stepped back with evident relief.

"Don't you like dancing?" David asked. "Or is there something my best friends haven't told me?"

The unexpected joke dissolved her tension. "I'm sorry," she apologised. "I do like dancing — or, at least, I used to. But Piers, my fiancé, didn't enjoy it, so I'm decidedly out of practice. He's my ex-fiancé now," she added, as they walked back to their table.

"I noticed you'd stopped wearing a ring," he said. "And recently, too. The mark hasn't faded. Who's Piers?"

"Piers Somerton, my boss."

"So that's why you left?"

"Yes," she said guardedly.

"Did you know him long?"

"Two and a half years."

"Who called it off?"

"He did. If it's any of your business."

"That's tough."

"As a matter of fact, it was mutual," she said coldly. "We had both been feeling for some time that it wasn't what we wanted, but not liking to hurt each other's feelings. He got over his qualms first, that's all."

"Still," David said, "I guess it shakes you up, when someone whose feelings you've taken for granted turns around and says, 'Thanks, but no thanks'. You start wondering how come you didn't read the signs right, and how many other times you got things wrong..."

He was right, she admitted to herself. It *had* been a blow to her self confidence, finding out the adoring Piers found her so very resistible after all.

"I don't particularly want to talk about it," she said.

"I'm sorry. I guess you're still upset?"

"No, I just don't feel it's a topic for general conversation. And it's been a long day. Is it all right if we go now?"

Immediately his manner became as distant as her own.

"Of course." He summoned a waiter with a casual nod, and left a cluster of notes on the table. "Do you want to wait in here while I pick up a taxi? The rank's a couple of hundred yards away."

"I don't mind walking to the rank." She would welcome the chance to cool her overheated cheeks, she thought. But as they came out into the shadowy street, the night air was chillier than she had expected. She could not suppress a shiver.

"You're cold," David said. "Have my jacket."

"No, thank you. I'm all right." Having insisted that she would not need to bring any warmer clothes, she felt a childish reluctance to admit that he had been right about the wisdom of bringing the despised cardigan.

"Please yourself," he said. The last vestiges of any fellow feeling between them seemed to have evaporated. They walked in silence along the road towards the distant lights and traffic of a main street. It really was quite cold. She hunched her shoulders and shivered again.

"Take the jacket," he said, as if to a child. "And stop being so damned proud."

He took off his dinner jacket and draped it round her shoulders. It had become pointless and undignified to argue, and the warmth of it was very welcome.

"Thank you," she said stiffly.

Once inside a taxi, she handed back the jacket. He took it without comment and folded it over his arm. When, after a silent ride, they reached her hotel, she felt ashamed of her ungracious behaviour. He had very kindly taken her out, as a favour to her father, and she had been prickly and ungrateful. It was hardly his fault if this strange girl he had been pressured into escorting was so mawkish and awkward that she couldn't behave with common civility in the company of a good-looking young man. She had snapped his head off every time one of his casual enquiries had touched her raw emotions, and he must be highly relieved that the difficult evening was over at last.

"Thank you for the meal," she said with a forced smile as he accompanied her to the hotel door. "It was very kind of you."

"Not at all. I enjoyed it. Parts of it."

"I'm sorry I was so touchy."

"It doesn't matter," he said politely. Then, unexpectedly, he grinned. "Though I'd say 'touchy' was an understatement. There were moments when it felt like having a conversation with a stick of TNT."

"I suppose it must have. I'm sorry," she said again.

"I guess we got off on the wrong foot.

It's been a bad day. Let's forget it and start again from square one. I'll see you in the morning."

"You don't have to — " she began.

"I know I don't have to. So what about it?"

"All right." Behind them, the taxi was waiting, its engine running. The driver revved impatiently.

"Good night," Jenny said, suddenly shy, her heart hammering.

"Good night," he said. There was an awkward kind of hiatus then he bent his head and kissed her, briefly, his hand momentarily cupping her chin. "I'll see you in the square, about nine o'clock," he called over his shoulder as he walked back to the taxi.

3

WHEN Jenny came out of the hotel a few minutes after nine o'clock the next morning, David Maine was sitting on a bench in the square, reading *L'Equipe*. He folded his paper away and stood up, and her heart started pounding all over again. His sports-jacketed figure could have stepped out of any of the glossy, designer-label shop windows they had passed on the previous day. Jenny was clad for practicality in a plain, oatmeal coloured cotton dress, because the day promised to be hot and sunny like yesterday, but she wished that the clothes she had brought with her were a bit more inspiring.

And what a waste to be in Paris without buying some new clothes in what was, after all, the fashion centre of the world. George had suggested she should 'go on the spree' . . . He probably felt mildly guilty about all those years of silence, and wanted to assuage his conscience with a few presents; he could certainly afford them. With that bitter thought running through her mind, she unconsciously lifted her chin, and her eyes took on a determined glint as she crossed the square.

"Good morning," David said politely. "Did you sleep well?"

"Yes, thank you. I was very comfortable. I hope you haven't been waiting long?"

"Just a few minutes. Have you anything planned for this morning?"

"I hadn't worked it out yet," Jenny said. "I thought of having a coffee in that bar-tabac on the corner and making some plans."

"Good idea," he said, falling into step beside her.

"Are you sure you can spare the time, though? Don't feel you have to, just because of George."

"Are you telling me to get lost?" he asked bluntly.

"No, of course not," Jenny said. "It

would be nice to have company. I just thought that as you seemed so busy yesterday — "

"Yesterday was short notice. Today I've got it fixed. If you want me to go away, say so and I'll go away. If you don't mind either way, I'll stay. So which is it to be?"

The question was so peremptory that she was tempted to say that she preferred to be alone. She actually opened her mouth to tell him so then changed her mind. He was maddening, but she had a feeling that without him her stay in Paris might be a confusing and lonely experience. He'd be a good guide to the city. She tried not to think of any other reasons for wanting him to stay.

"Well, if it really isn't too much of a nuisance — " she began, then caught his exasperated, heavenward glance and finished quickly, "Thank you."

"That's settled, then."

"With coffees, black and aromatic, on the circular metal table in front of them, they sat in the sun while the population of Passy went about its morning business.

Everyone seemed energetic and purposeful and cheerfully garrulous. Her spirits lifted as the magic of Paris began to reach her senses, and she smiled at David over the top of her coffee cup.

"I'm not surprised you fell for this city. It's so lively."

He returned her grin. "Lady, you ain't seen nuthin' yet," he replied, with a broad mock-Brooklyn accent. "But it *is* infectious, isn't it? Well, what about plans for this morning, or do you want another cup of coffee first?"

"I'd just like to wander round a bit first. See some of the famous, obvious things, like the Eiffel Tower of course, and the Seine and the bridges, and do some shopping. But I'm really supposed to be working, checking on some details of research for my father."

"What exactly does he want you to do?"

"I have a list here." She produced the

slim envelope from her handbag. The neatly typed list of required information was only a few pages long. David glanced through it briefly.

"Well, that doesn't look too arduous. The *Conciergerie*: save that for a rainy day when you're feeling depressed already. It can be quite chilling standing in the rooms where they kept the prisoners before they were guillotined. The Louvre: same applies. It's so big, it's exhausting so don't waste your first day and this sunshine. The *Musée de la Marine*: that's easy, and quite near here. We could go there this morning if you're feeling virtuous and want to make a start. Versailles is an all-day affair, because of the queues and because it's out of town. I'll drive you there one day if you like, or there's a train if you prefer to go alone."

"I think the first thing I'd better do is buy a map."

"Here you are." He produced a small, maroon-bound volume from his pocket. "*Plan de Paris*. Now, as far as transport is concerned, the car is not far from here, in one of the underground parks, but if you don't mind the Métro, it's a lot quicker and simpler. You can get a tourist ticket for unlimited travel."

"The Métro it is, then."

She was glad to have David with her in the noisy ticket queue. In the tiled passageways, the babble of conversation was magnified and largely incomprehensible. A thin, serious girl played the violin to a taped orchestral accompaniment, in one of the broad corridors leading to the trains. At her feet, and inside the battered violin case, passers-by had left coins. She seemed oblivious to her audience, and her playing was of a high standard. Passing her, David dropped a coin in the velvet bed of the case, but she didn't alter her concentrated stare. "She's probably a student at the *Conservatoire*," he informed Jenny, as they descended the concrete stairs to the platform. "They use the Métro as a practice hall, and pick up pocket money at the same time."

Jenny stalked into the *Musée* ahead of him. During the two hours they spent wandering around the polished wooden floors of the maritime museum, Jenny assiduously took notes. Enormous paintings of sea battles and great ships lined the walls, many of them painted, according to the notices by which they were accompanied, as presents from a grateful king of France to his ministers and favoured subjects. There were glass cases full of the assorted naval equipment of centuries, and salvaged cannons and painted figureheads, and an audio-visual display tracing the development of the sailing ship from slave galley to clipper. The star attractions of the museum were the scale models of ships, accurate in every detail, which had been constructed to demonstrate to one of the Dauphins the intricacies of shipbuilding, and the details of maritime routine.

"This is beautiful," Jenny breathed, standing beside a huge model of the *Louis Quinze*. George had asked for details of the age of the original ship, the number of guns, the crew, the ornaments. She wrote rapidly in her notebook. David strolled away to other exhibits, then returned to glance over her shoulder.

"I'm surprised he needs all this information. I could have sworn he took down all the details he needed when he was here, last year."

"Apparently not," Jenny said.

"He took home a briefcase full of books and pamphlets from the museum bookshop, and he also made all those notes you're making now. I was with him."

"I suppose he must have lost them, then."

"That's not like George. Anyway, why send you? He knew I was here. He could have phoned me for some duplicate information. It's odd that he didn't."

"You'd better take it up with him," Jenny said coldly. "I just do what I'm asked." She was nettled by the casual inference that her work could have been more efficiently carried out by the great

David Maine, and she didn't want him looking over her shoulder and making her hand wobble as she worked. It was infuriating that her treacherous body couldn't stop reacting to his nearness, distracting her constantly by registering the details of his face, the line of his neck and shoulders as he stood close to her, the shape of his wrist and hand lightly holding the notebook steady as he studied her notes. She was relieved when he left her to it, and she was able to concentrate on the job in hand.

When she had finished, it was almost one o'clock. They had lunch at a pavement café within sight of the Eiffel Tower. "The prices are a rip-off," David said, "but it's easier than trekking off to a less touristy area. I sincerely hope you don't want to go up the tower? Not right now, anyway."

"No, not right now. I don't think my legs could take much more, after standing in the museum all morning. But I shall have to go up some time before I go home. It's more or less obligatory for first-time visitors, isn't it?"

David groaned, but admitted that the view was good. "We'll pencil it in for another day, then, unless you come to your senses. So what shall we do this afternoon? You said something about shopping. There's the Boulevard Hausseman area, which is the Paris equivalent of Oxford Street, or the flea markets or, if you want something really up-market, there are the designer shops like Lanvin and St. Laurent in the arcades around the Champs-Elysées, or along the Rue de Rivoli near the Louvre."

"I'm not sure I have the energy for shopping," Jenny said regretfully, easing her feet in the not-very-practical high-heeled shoes she had chosen that morning for looks instead of comfort, in preference to her paint-spattered trainers.

"Then how about a trip on one of the *bateaux-mouches*, the ferry boats that go down the Seine, under the bridges? It's another tourist essential, which you may as well get out of the way, and it would be quite pleasant on the water on a warm afternoon like this. The Champs-Elysées galleries are open until late in the evening, so you can look at those later, if your energy returns."

"That sounds marvellous," Jenny said.

They found places on a cushioned bench at the rear of one of the big passenger boats which operated from the Pont D'Iena, close to the Eiffel Tower.

The river wind ruffled David's dark hair and blew long, auburn strands of Jenny's across her face as the boat forged upstream towards the Ile de la Cité and Nôtre Dame. Barely audible above the engines of the boat, a taped commentary in four languages droned on, describing the history of the buildings on either bank. David, of course, must have heard it all before. She got the impression that he was watching her rather than the scenery. He had taken off his jacket, and was leaning back against the padded bench seat with his shirt sleeved right arm draped casually behind her. If she leaned back herself she would be brushing against it. She sat stiffly upright, concentrating on the taped voice and the scenes on the river bank, until she noticed a man, a photographer, passing down the rows of seats and taking snapshots of the passengers. He halted in front of them.

"*Monsieur, Mademoiselle, vous êtes ensemble?*"

David agreed that, yes, they were together.

"*Si vous pouvez embracer vôtre petite amie, Monsieur ça fera un bon photo.*"

"*Comme ça?*" David's arm came round her, firmly hooking her against him. The camera clicked, twice. The photographer moved on, but David's arm remained around Jenny's shoulders. She felt a confusion of reactions. On the other hand, the sensation in itself was pleasant, to say the least. She would have liked to relax against his shoulder . . . On the one hand, he hadn't so much as touched her until the photographer arrived, and most probably didn't mean anything by it now. While she was still wondering how to react, the hand on her shoulder as casually transferred itself back to the bench seat. When she stole a sideways glance at him through her lashes, he was watching the Palais de Justice sliding past on the left bank, his expression unreadable.

When the boat came back to the Pont D'Iena at the end of a forty-minute trip, the photographer sprang ashore first and began to pin up rows of ready-developed snapshots on a board by the gangplank. Most of the passengers who disembarked bought a copy.

David paused by the board. "Do you want one?" She looked at the pictures. Both of them had come out well. They had caught her shy, startled look as the camera clicked. David, looking straight into the lens, had that unfathomable expression on his face but she had to admit that he was photogenic as well as good-looking. At the memory of those few seconds of contact her stomach contracted. The photographer was sliding the two snapshots into cardboard folders. David handed one to Jenny and stowed the other in his pocket without comment.

They strolled up the tree-lined esplanade toward the Pont D'Iena, with the huge bulk of the Eiffel Tower looming over it. On the bridge, street traders had spread out blankets on which to display their wares: beads and tooled leather handbags and bright paper birds with some kind of mechanism which at the pull of a string sent them swooping and soaring over the heads of passers-by. A stall at the foot of the bridge was selling posters of high-kicking chorus girls and can-can dancers, cheap copies of the famous Toulouse-Lautrec advertisements for the cabaret at the *Moulin Rouge*. There was a scratchy portable gramophone on the stall, playing samples of a stack of LPs labelled 'The Music of Paris', a jumble of flute and hurdy-gurdy and singing violin which seemed to reflect the happy mood of the surroundings:

the paper birds, the jostling crowds, the roar of traffic, sunlight glinting on the river and on the glossy backs of careless cosmopolitan pigeons, who pecked among the feet of pedestrians for crumbs of picnic baguettes and *pain-au-chocolat*. Jenny found that she was walking in time to the music, swinging along at David's side, and that there was a smile on her face. She remembered the words of a song she had once heard.

'... I'm in love with Paris ...

I get the Paris fever,

Joie de vivre.'

Paris fever was a good way to describe it, she thought. A feeling of being lightheaded and alive and ready for something special to happen.

"Got your energy back?" David asked.

"Oh, yes. What about the Eiffel Tower, now we're here? It seems a shame to miss the chance." They were only about fifty yards away from one of the colossal supports. He pulled a mock-agonised face. "Oh, come on," she coaxed, touching his arm. "You said the view was good, didn't you?"

He looked down at her bright face and sparkling eyes, and suddenly the mood between them changed. "The view looks pretty good from here, too." There was a new, husky note in his voice, and her knees felt weak as she saw the expression on his face. He took her by the shoulders and drew her gently towards him. It seemed inevitable that he should kiss her. She tilted her face. The first touch of his mouth was tentative, then his lips returned searchingly. She instinctively responded as his hands moved, pulling her closer, deepening the kiss. Her lips parted, her own hands spreading across his back. Under the thin shirt, his shoulder blades were hard and warm against her palms. When they moved apart, she felt dazzled and breathless, and newly sensitive in every part of her body. As she opened her eyes, tenderness flooding through her, she found, with a shock, that he was smiling — not with responsive tenderness, but with wary, cynical amusement.

"Well . . . " he said, teasingly. "It looks like you *are* a true Acre after all. Crabby exterior, and a real soft centre."

Jenny broke away. He was so infuriatingly sure of himself. Her moment of weakness evaporated. Damn the man! But it was her own fault, for letting the flush of Paris fever betray her into dropping her guard.

"I wouldn't be so sure about the soft centre," she told him cuttingly. "Was it part of George's instructions to throw in a romantic clinch or two along with the Métro tickets?"

"No," he said. "That was my idea. You seemed to think it was a pretty good one at the time."

"I hesitate to puncture your self-esteem but, on reflection, you clearly have so much of the stuff that I need not concern myself. I can't imagine what you base it on, mind you!"

"Come off it," he said, stung by the contemptuous barb. "The kiss was fifty-fifty, you can't pretend it wasn't. And when it comes to self-esteem — "

Suddenly there was a screech of brakes as a car swung across from the stream of traffic flowing over the bridge and ground to a halt an inch from the kerb beside them. There was a chorus of indignant hooting and Gallic insults from the drivers of other cars which had had to swerve or brake sharply as a result of this unheralded manoeuvre.

The car was a sleek Mercedes in a glittering shade of electric blue. The driver was a man in his late thirties, with a bony, hawklike face beneath waving fair hair. He seemed totally unperturbed by the chaos he had just caused. Behind him, the passenger's window on the pavement side hissed downwards with electronic smoothness.

"David! What luck to see you. I've been trying to ring you for two whole days. Where have you been hiding?"

The voice was strong, deep and throatily feminine, with a distinct American drawl. The speaker was wearing enormous, fashionable sunglasses and a wide-brimmed straw hat, from beneath which flowed a mane of elaborately waved and teased out blonde hair. Her eyes were hidden by the sunglasses, but the rest of her face was perfectly made-up, from the precise outline of her flossy crimson lips to the blusher heavily accenting her high cheekbones. She was not young, probably in her mid-forties, but she was intensely glamorous, and her manner suggested that she knew it.

David didn't look thrilled to see her.

"Oh. Hi, Angela," he said, after a moment's hesitation. "Sorry if you've had trouble getting in touch. I've been a bit tied up for the last couple of days."

"So I see," Angela purred sweetly, turning the bland surfaces of her sunglasses on Jenny. "But, darling, you might have let me know."

"I did. I phoned yesterday. Didn't you get my message?"

"I did tell you about David's phone call yesterday," murmured the car driver. Although the accent was French, he spoke quickly in what was apparently fluent English.

"Did you? Oh yes. But it was rather terse, though, wasn't it, darling?" She turned back to David. "Anyway, the reason I've been trying to get in touch with you was that I wanted you to come over this afternoon. There's something I wanted to tell you about."

David spread his hands apologetically. "Sorry, Angela, I can't. I'm busy this afternoon. Oh, by the way, let me introduce you to Jenny Chatham, who's here in Paris for a short vacation. You know her father, I think — George Acre."

"Oh, yes. The writer." Angela studied Jenny, her expression disconcertingly masked by those enormous sunglasses. "Have you been here long?"

"Just since yesterday."

" . . . And Jenny, this is Angela Torrance." Clearly the name was supposed to mean something, and it did seem vaguely familiar although she couldn't quite remember why.

"Jenny's over here doing a spot of

research on George's behalf, and I said I'd take her round and show her the sights," David explained, making her sound, Jenny thought, like a small child on a day trip.

"Well, that's very king of you, David, but do you have to desert me utterly? What I want to talk about won't keep forever. Just how long is your friend going to be here?"

"A week, isn't it Jenny?"

"That's right. I go back in another five days, next Sunday."

"But that's ages! Can't we go back to my place now? Bring Jenny along too if you want. She can have a swim and talk to Marcel while you and I catch up. She won't mind, will you, honey?"

Angela clearly wasn't used to being denied. She opened the rear passenger door. The car engine was still running. David looked at Jenny.

"Would you mind?"

"No, of course not," she said stiffly. "Or, if you prefer, you can leave me here. I'm sure I can find my way back to the hotel."

The driver leaned over and opened his door, too. He looked up at her engagingly. Fine lines radiated from the corners of his eyes as he smiled.

"Why not come along? I would be delighted to take David's place as your companion while he is busy. Please don't disappoint me."

The charm was blatant, almost a caricature of the amorous Frenchman of the popular image, but it was also appealing.

"Oh, do come on, darlings, before a gendarme turns up and arrests us all for snarling up the traffic system," drawled Angela impatiently. David half-pushed the hesitating Jenny into the front of the car beside the driver, then he himself climbed into the back with Angela Torrance. The Mercedes revved aggressively and, with hair-raising disregard for the niceties of the highway code, pulled out again into the stream of traffic.

4

ANGELA TORRANCE'S 'place' turned out to be a pink-washed stucco manor house, almost a small château, a few miles outside Paris on the outskirts of a village of shuttered, shingle-roofed houses and stony trackways. The only road, which had passed between miles of cultivated farmland, ran through the village, skirted the edge of a small wood, ran alongside a high boundary wall and came to an end in front of a great pair of intricately wrought-iron gates, standing between tall brick pillars topped with stone lions.

If the gates were impressive, the view of the old house, standing at the end of a long, raked gravel avenue of cedar trees, was even more so. There seemed to be countless long windows flanked by faded wooden shutters and topped by delicately moulded architraves. The gracious façade was beautiful and a little shabby, although the gardens surrounding the house were immaculately kept with complicated topiary birds topping the clipped yew hedges that flanked the house, and marble statues on stone-paved terraces above the rose beds.

"Well, home at last," said Angela, gliding out of the car in a movement which showed a lot of slim, bronzed leg. She led the way through an archway into a cool, paved courtyard where a central fountain splashed peacefully into a stone basin lined with mosaic tiles, and a great peach tree, trained like a fan against a south-facing wall, drank up the late afternoon sunshine.

Angela strolled into the cool, darkened interior of the house, where the curtains were drawn to keep the sun off the shining wood of antique furnishings. "Dominic," she called. "Drinks at once, please, in the courtyard. With plenty of ice." Marcel had driven the car to the garage block behind the house. Jenny looked around her with awe.

"Does all of this belongs to Angela?"

"No," David said. "She rents it from a slightly down-at-heel viscount. He's off economising in Biarritz, praying that she won't deface the family heirlooms. Are you sure you don't mind about coming along? I left Angela a message yesterday to say I would be busy for the next week, but she's not an easy person to put off."

"No, I don't mind. I've never been anywhere as stately-home as this, except as a gawping tripper," Jenny admitted ingenuously. "It's very impressive. Do you have business with Angela?"

"That's right," David said, without elaborating.

Angela came out of the house again, her expensive lawn dress, in vibrant, geometric panels of colour, floating around her model-slim figure. She had removed the sunglasses momentarily to show elaborately painted eyes under mascara-laden lashes.

"Sit down, you guys. The drinks are on their way." She sank down languorously on a cushioned stone seat under one of the windows and ran a carefully careless hand through her mass of blonde waves.

"Wow, it's been so incredibly warm today, don't you think?" she murmured, giving David a seductive look which entirely excluded Jenny. He went to sit beside her and Jenny perched awkwardly on the broad stone brim of the fountain, trailing her fingers in the cool water.

Angela fanned herself with her crimson-tipped hands and continued, "Am I exhausted! I've been trailing round the dress shops all afternoon, trying to find something to wear for tomorrow evening, but everything was so boring. You cannot believe how tedious the fashions are this year — everything was so dull! Oh, David that reminds me, I just have to have you with me tomorrow night. It's *very* important. You won't let me down, will you darling? It's Hank Henderson's party."

"It's a bit difficult," he demurred. "I

had something else planned for tomorrow night." He did not say whether his plans included Jenny. "Can't Marcel take you?"

"Darling, Marcel is very obliging, but I can't go to Hank Henderson's party with my *secretary* for heaven's sake! Everyone knows Marcel. No, it just has to be some mysterious, alluring, gorgeous young man . . . that's you, isn't it?" And she captured his brown hand and held it possessively in both of hers, snuggling against him on the bench. He looked embarrassed but did not pull away.

"Please, darling . . . as a special favour?" she wheedled. Jenny felt more and more uncomfortable. Angela was now tickling the back of David's neck with her hand and blowing in his ear, as if Jenny wasn't there.

"All right," David said hastily. "Cut it out, will you, Angela?" But he said it with a friendly, familiar intonation which took away the rejection implicit in the words. "I'll go to the darn party, if it's that important."

"Thanks a million honey. I knew you wouldn't turn me down. Hey," she discovered, lifting his hand again and turning it to examine the enamel cufflinks set in the blue fabric of the shirt. "You're not wearing those gold cufflinks I bought you. Why not? Didn't you like them?"

"Yes, of course I did. They were very stylish. But you shouldn't give me things like that, Angie."

"Why not? What's wrong with a little birthday present?"

"In the first place, Cartier cufflinks are not a *little* birthday present, and in the second place, it didn't happen to be my birthday."

"Aw, don't bother me wid details," Angela drawled, in a passable imitation of James Cagney's nasal accents. "I like giving presents. Don't spoil an old woman's simple pleasures." But the look she was giving David was not in the least old-womanly. Jenny stared down into the water, wondering if she had the nerve to get up and demand to phone for a taxi back to her hotel. She didn't want to hang around cramping Angela Torrance's style any longer — not, it had to be admitted, that Angela showed the least sign of being cramped!

A dark-suited butler brought out a tray of drinks, pale and bubbling, with ice cubes clinking in the long-stemmed glasses, just as Marcel reappeared through the archway.

"Ah, Marcel. Just in time for the booze, as always." Angela gestured with a languid hand. "Help yourself. And then I want you to show Jenny the pool and keep her entertained while David and I have our little *tête-a-tête.*"

"I've no swimming things," Jenny said stiffly.

"No problem, darling. I have heaps of spare things for guests. Marcel will fix you up, won't you darling?" Angela bestowed that word on everyone, but with David she seemed to give it an extra throaty quality. She picked up a glass for David and one for herself and led him away, leaving Jenny feeling a powerful dislike for her.

Marcel did not seem at all averse to her company. He was flatteringly attentive, asking her questions about herself, his dark eyes fixed on her as they sipped their drinks. Gradually, his interest, and his warm, attractive voice, forced her to relax and she found herself telling him what he wanted to know about her trip to Paris, about her home and work, and her famous father, George Acre, the best-selling novelist.

"And what about you? Have you known Angela long?" she asked.

He calculated. "Five months. It is almost five months since I have begun to work for her."

"What do you do?" Angela had called him her secretary.

He smiled. "I am everything. Secretary, chauffeur — what do you call it? — 'bouncer' on occasion, when there is someone around that she does not wish to see. I deal with the Press when they are troublesome. And when she is sad, if there is no one better available, I hold her hand."

"I knew I recognised her face from somewhere," Jenny said. "But I couldn't remember where. From what you say, she is obviously famous."

"I am glad that Angela did not hear you say that," Marcel said, with feeling. "She would be furious to think that you do not recognise her immediately. She is an actress, and her greatest success has been in a television soap opera. It is made in America but it is a *succès fou*, a big hit, all over the word. It is called 'Prairie' and it is about the cattle barons of Texas."

"Yes, of course," Jenny said quickly. "I remember now. She plays the second wife of the chief cattle baron, doesn't she? I have seen it, but not very often . . . I don't watch a lot of television," she added apologetically. She *had* turned the programme on once, by accident, and hated it.

"I expect a beautiful girl like you finds more interesting things to do with her time," Marcel said lightly, giving her a glance which would have been described, she thought, as smouldering. But he *was* nice, and it was pleasant, even exciting, to flirt with a distinguished-looking Frenchman in an idyllic garden on a summer afternoon . . .

The sparkling wine must have gone to her head a little, she realised suddenly. Marcel had left his seat, and come to sit beside her on the fountain edge. He was disconcertingly close. "Angela said something about a swim, didn't she?" Jenny asked hastily, trying to ignore the fact of his proximity. Her voice came out on a note of panic. At once he stood up, friendly and polite, and in no way threatening.

"Of course. Come with me and we'll find you a costume."

He led her through the archway, past an immaculately clipped hedge and into the pool garden, where an enormous swimming pool, surrounded by dense yew hedging, sparkled invitingly. It was luxuriously tiled with mosaics depicting what looked like a full-blown Roman orgy glimmering through the blue water. At one end, a semicircular shallow bay, surrounded by imitation Doric Columns, contained a fountain in which a nude bronze nymph with a mournful expression poured water endlessly from a raised pitcher. Placed at intervals around the pool were deeply-cushioned lounging chairs. The whole scene was immensely redolent of Hollywood, and at odds with the gracious old house to which it belonged. Jenny found it hard to equate the pool with a hard-up *vicomte* and family heirlooms. Perhaps, she thought, the pool had been built purely in order to make the house more appealing to rich overseas tenants like Angela Torrance.

Marcel showed her to a changing room like a miniature Greek temple, with the arches glazed in and heavily curtained in thick muslin fabric. There were shelves around the room piled high with assorted swimwear and thick Turkish towels.

"There should be something here to suit you," he said, and left her to it.

There were at least a dozen swimsuits to choose from, but they were all two-piece all more stylish, expensive and revealing than anything she would have bought for herself. Eventually, she found a plain brown bikini, marginally less skimpy than the jungle-printed, exotic scraps of fabric which Angela seemed to favour. Even so, when she tried it on, it covered up much less of herself than Piers would have considered decent.

She came out of the building, swinging a towel, to find David talking to Marcel who had already changed into swimming trunks and a towelling robe. They both stopped in mid-sentence and stared at her. It was rather gratifying. Then Marcel gave a long-drawn-out whistle.

"Fantastic!"

"Very nice," David said drily. "Look, I'm going to be busy for a while. Would you mind if Marcel takes you back to the hotel — when you've had your swim, of course?" He glanced at his watch. "I'll try to pick you up at eight, to take you out to supper. It's five-thirty now. I may be a little late — "

"Don't worry about that," Marcel broke in smoothly. "I can take Jenny to supper. I would be delighted to have the honour." His eyes were on her as he spoke.

"That's OK, Marcel, it won't be necessary. I should be through by eight," David said, coldly. "If not, Jenny, I'll give you a ring to let you know when I'm coming."

He took it for granted that she would wait, Jenny thought, indignantly. And he had turned down Marcel's offer on her behalf, without, apparently, the slightest realisation that Marcel had been inviting *her*, not merely offering to fill in for David. "Thank you, Marcel, I'd love to have supper with you," she said, sweetly. "That will save you having to rush your business with Angela on my behalf," she added to David, who looked taken aback. Clearly he was surprised by the ease with which she was ready to relinquish an evening of his company.

From somewhere near the house a voice, Angela's, called, "David? Where are you? Do hurry."

"Duty calls," Marcel murmured wickedly. David sighed and ran a hand through his hair. He looked harrassed.

"Coming," he called. "Look, Marcel, I'd like a quick word with Jenny. Can you tell Angela I'm on my way?"

Marcel strolled away towards the distant voice. David waited until he was out of earshot, then turned to Jenny. He seemed to have got over his initial tendency to stare at the parts of her that weren't covered with swimsuit.

"I'd better warn you," he said quietly, "watch your step with Marcel. He's apt to make a pass at anything in a skirt."

"Even me?" Jenny said, in mock amazement. "Well, that's all right. I'm not wearing a skirt, as even you seem to have noticed."

David let out an exasperated breath. "Seriously — " he began.

"This may come as a terrible shock to you," Jenny continued, with mounting resentment, "But I am not a naı:ve schoolgirl. I am twenty-three years old, and not totally without experience of men."

"All right," David snapped back. "I'm sorry I opened my big mouth. Carry right on. But Marcel doesn't bother with women unless it's for one of two things: money, or sex. Now, it's fairly obvious that you're not in his league financially, unless, that is, you've been dropping little hints about your rich Daddy . . . which leaves sex."

It was close to the bone, that comment about her father's money. "It seems to me," Jenny said, acidly, "that you are the one who should be worried. Judging by the way that Angela was crawling all over you a while back, she'd like to eat you whole, right down to your shoes and not forgetting your Cartier cufflinks, if only you'd worn them."

She had raised her voice in indignation, and he stepped forward, dropping a restraining hand on her shoulder. "Shh," he said urgently. "She'll hear you."

Jenny twisted away from his hand. "I

don't care! I think you've got the most almighty nerve. One minute you dump me on Marcel for the evening, and the next you warn me against him! What am I supposed to do about it?" His hands closed on her upper arms and he shook her angrily.

"Will you be quiet? I did *not* dump you, as you so elegantly put it. He offered, and you leapt at the chance, with such alacrity that I thought I'd better tell you to put the brakes on, that's all. But if you want to be an easy conquest for that Gallic romeo, that's your affair."

She stared at him, outraged. "Oh . . . you . . . you . . . I don't think I've ever met anybody so — "

"So what?" he challenged, still gripping her bare arms.

"So intolerable!"

"You seemed to tolerate me pretty well this morning," he said softly. "Remember?"

Jenny shook herself free, stepped back and delivered him a stinging blow, open handed, across the cheek. She regretted it instantly. There was a long moment while he stared at her, the mark of the blow livid on his skin. He looked white round the mouth, and dangerous. Jenny's stomach tightened and her hands clenched into fists at her sides. "I am perfectly capable," she said, with a bravado she was far from feeling, "of fending off any unwanted passes."

David's breath was coming fast, as if he had been running. His eyes were densely blue. "Are you?" he said conversationally. "Let's find out, shall we?" And as she brought her fists up, she found her wrists caught and held behind her, so that in a moment she was pinned against his chest as his mouth came down hard on hers, invading, demanding a response.

Her resistance ebbed. It wasn't just David she had to fight, it was herself. With an intensity that shocked her, she wanted to give way, to subside into his arms, kiss him in return, soften and tame his anger and convert it into the kind of kiss he had given her that afternoon on the

Pont D'Iena. She had never felt such a hungry response to a man — not to the serious schoolboys of her teenage romances, nor to the numerous young men to whom she had been briefly attracted during her university days, and certainly not to Piers. It nearly overturned her senses. But that was what he expected, and was waiting for. He relaxed his hold, just a little, sensing her weakening, and the momentary respite restored her determination not to let him win this encounter. Her body stiffened.

At that, he let her go unexpectedly, and she almost fell.

"Well, if that was unwanted," he told her mockingly, "you should try not to look so inviting."

Jenny brushed a shaking hand across her mouth. "Have you quite finished demonstrating your superior male power? Has it begun to occur to you that maybe it wasn't you I was looking inviting *for*?"

David straightened up, his eyes widening. He shook his head fractionally, like a boxer after receiving a blow. Quite suddenly the anger, and the confidence, drained out of him.

"Oh, heck . . . " he said, under his breath. "Look, I'm sorry. Did I hurt you?"

"You must be joking," Jenny retorted, half in tears. She rubbed furiously at her bruised wrists.

"I'm sorry," he said, again helplessly. "I misread the situation. It seems to be a common failing of mine. I promise it won't happen again . . . Will you accept an apology?"

She was still shaking, and still stubbornly determined to show that she couldn't be taken for granted. But the concern in his eyes shook her resolve. She took a step towards him. "Yes, I accept." she said gently. "And I'm sorry I hit you."

He gave a rueful snort of laughter. "So am I," he admitted. "You pack quite a punch. Ever thought of being a contender?"

Jenny grinned back, warmth flooding

through her. It was crazy, she thought, how many times, in the twenty-four hours or so since she had met this maddening man, she had swung from detesting him to a completely opposite emotion. Well, at least a day with David Maine could not be dull!

"David! Are you going to be all *night?*" The plaintive voice was Angela's, and getting close.

"I'd better go," David said. "Enjoy your evening."

Marcel came back a few minutes later and they swam a few brisk lengths of the pool. Jenny was trying to shut the episode of the last few minutes out of her mind. She felt confused. Her feelings for David Maine, when he was no longer there to melt her resolve, were an untenable mixture of liking and mistrust, of strong physical attraction and the realisation that it was not safe to drop her guard when dealing with a man like him. If she was in this highly-charged state within a mere day of his company, what kind of an emotional tangle could she get herself into by the end of a week? And she didn't need that kind of trouble with a man at this stage of her life. If only he wasn't so disturbing, she could think straight... She smiled and swam and splashed with Marcel, and admired his highly efficient crawl and his streamlined diving with the secure feeling that whatever David had said, Marcel at least did not pose any kind of emotional threat.

When Jenny had changed back into her clothes and Marcel was ready to drive her back to her hotel, she wondered whether perhaps she should say goodbye to Angela, her less-than-gracious hostess.

"Better not disturb her," Marcel advised. "If she is with David, she does not like to be interrupted."

"But surely she doesn't need any more antiques? This house is ready furnished, isn't it?"

"What makes you think that he is selling her antiques?" Marcel asked, the suspicion of a smile hovering at the corners of his mouth.

"He said they had a business connection." Jenny was bothered by Marcel's knowing expression.

"Business? I suppose you could say that . . . he hasn't explained about Angela, then?"

"No," Jenny said. It almost sounded as if he was suggesting that they were having an affair. Or worse, something less straightforward . . .

Marcel was watching her closely. "Are you in love with David?" he asked.

"No, of course not. I only met him yesterday. I hardly know him."

"I am glad to hear it," Marcel said gravely.

Jenny waited on the gravel at the front of the house for Marcel to bring the car round from the garage. After a while she had a sensation of being watched. She scanned the blank faces of the windows and thought she saw a glimpse of someone half-concealed behind the curtains of one of the downstairs rooms. As the Mercedes crunched to a halt on the gravel, a little girl of seven or eight, wide-eyed and solemn, dressed in an expensive, brightly-patterned smock which didn't suit her, ran out from the main entrance and down the steps towards the car.

"Marcel! Where are you going? You promised to swim with me this afternoon."

"Sorry, *Chérie*," Marcel said, easily. "I have to do something else now. I will swim with you tomorrow, I promise."

The girl pulled a disappointed face. "That's what you said yesterday. I'll never get to swim at this rate. Mom won't let me go near the pool alone. You know she won't."

Marcel shrugged. "I cannot help it, little one. Why don't you ask Dominic or Céline to accompany you?"

"They're all busy," the girl said sadly. She kicked at the gravel with the toe of her expensive shoe. "Everyone's always busy here."

"Shame," Marcel consoled, putting the car into gear. "Go and watch TV or something."

"Poor little thing," Jenny said as they

drove away. "Shouldn't you have stayed, if you promised?"

"It is not my job to look after Laurie," Marcel said casually.

"Who is she?"

"Angela's daughter. She is here for a few weeks. Normally there is a governess but the woman is ill, which is a great nuisance because no one else has the time to look after the child. She needs children of her own age to play with, but Angela will not permit that the village children come to the house because she is responsible for the furniture, which is very valuable, and there is no one to supervise."

"Poor thing," Jenny said again, remembering the girl's hurt, lonely expression.

"Oh, she is not so badly off. David takes her out sometimes, when he is not so busy. At other times she comes with me, or amuses herself. Anyway, soon she will go back to her father in California for a visit."

"Angela's husband?"

"For the time being, yes. They are in the middle of a divorce. At the moment, until it is arranged with which of them she will live, she goes from one to the other, for two months at a time.

So Laurie was another sad child being passed between divorcing parents. Jenny was haunted by the memory of the little girl's face, the set of her shoulders, her shoe aimlessly kicking at the gravel as she passed her time among strangers and a mother who didn't seem to bother with her. Perhaps there was something Jenny could do for her — take her out, or offer to keep her company? The problem was that this might be seen as intruding unasked into Angela's household. It would be difficult to achieve tactfully, but she determined to try.

For the rest of the evening, Marcel was a witty and charming companion. The restaurant he chose was as delightful, and the food as deliciously varied, as that of the previous evening, but Jenny found it extremely hard to concentrate, with her mind wandering constantly between the problem of Angela's lonely little girl and the memory of David Maine's kiss beside the swimming pool.

Marcel didn't seem to mind her frequent silences, but kept her amused, when her attention was not wandering, with anecdotes about acquaintances, about restaurants he had visited, and disastrous moments during his short but eventful career as Angela Torrance's personal assistant. To her relief, despite David's warning, he showed no inclination to make the kind of pass at her that she had rashly assured David she could handle. He was attentive and flattering, and made it clear that she attracted him but he kept at a reassuring distance. It was not until the end of the evening, when he had driven her back to the hotel, that he captured her hands and looked at her seriously.

"I have very much enjoyed this evening, Jenny. May I see you again?"

"I . . . I don't know. That is, I am supposed to be working for my father while I am in Paris. But I did enjoy this evening, too. Thank you."

"Ah, yes. The research for the book. Perhaps I could help with that?"

"Won't you be busy, working for Angela?"

"She will not be needing me tomorrow night," he reminded her, "because she will be going to a party with David. So I will have time off. Would you like to go to the party with me? I can get an invitation. It is at the house of some very rich friends of Angela, who are in the movie business. They are staying in the eighth arrondissement, in an apartment close to the *Nissom de Camondo* museum in the Rue de Monceau." The museum was on her father's list, Jenny remembered. "It should be a good party. They are immensely rich."

Jenny wondered fleetingly what David would think of her arrival at the party in the company of Marcel. He could hardly object — he, after all, would be escorting the man-eating Angela Torrance. She was very tempted to go if only to see the expression on his face when she swanned in on Marcel's arm . . . and, of course, she told herself sternly, because Marcel was pleasant, and charming, and it would be a delightful way to spend another of her few evenings in Paris. There was, however one very real problem. Her peridot silk outfit just would not do in the company of Angela and her jet-set friends.

"I would love to go to the party," she told Marcel. "But will it be very grand? I would have to buy something to wear."

"Is that a problem?"

"Oh, no. My father said I could get some clothes while I was here. But I don't know where to begin to look for special things, suitable for a jet-set party," she explained.

"Why don't I take you shopping tomorrow afternoon? I know all the best places," Marcel offered. "There are many beautiful shops in the galleries off the Champs-Elysées where you can pick up something from the ready-to-wear ranges as there is no time to order something from a couturier."

Jenny remembered that David had spoken of the Champs-Elysées galleries as very up-market. She felt a little shaken. Marcel had suggested that they would make an adequate substitute for 'something from a couturier'. Had he misunderstood her careless remarks about her father's generosity? Well, she would just have to disillusion him. Tomorrow.

5

THE phone beside her bed rang early, as Jenny was finishing her coffee and croissants at the small table by the window in her room. David's voice on the line sounded carefully casual.

"Hi, Jenny. Did you have a good evening?"

"Yes, thank you," she said, not going into details. She wished that she could stop feeling so hot and cold and shaky at the mere sound of his voice.

"Are you busy this morning? I have to go to the *Louvre des Antiquaires* to see a man about a bureau. I thought you might find it interesting."

Jenny was silent. She imagined him at the other end of a telephone line, waiting for her answer, and the image of his lean, cleanly-cut profile and quizzical expression was so clear in her memory that it hurt. She sat down on the bed, trying to steady her reactions. 'Oh, you're pathetic!' she berated herself. 'If he knew, he'd find you ridiculous. He probably does, anyway.'

"I promise to behave," David said lightly into the silence. "No mauling."

"What exactly is the *Louvre des Antiquaires*?" She hoped her detailed recall of the previous 'mauling' wasn't betrayed by her voice.

"It's a building close to the *Palais Royale*, entirely devoted to antiques and jewellery — a kind of antique-dealers' Harrods," he explained. "Everything on display is top quality. It's like a museum, only in some respects it's better, because you get the feeling that if you ever became *really* rich, you could actually own the stuff, and for another thing, as it's all for sale it gets polished more often. It's quite a place."

"It sounds marvellous," Jenny said. "Yes, I'd like to come."

He met her in the square and they went by Métro. Neither of them made any reference to the events of the previous day.

The *Louvre des Antiquaires* was as fascinating as he had suggested it would be: dozens of glazed-in shop areas on three floors, lining corridors of glistening parquet. Red escalators carried the customers between floors. When they were tired, stylish black lounging chairs, dotted around the central marbled squares, gave them a chance to think over prospective purchases. The shops were a dazzle of beautiful, desirable artefacts: paintings, bronzes, carvings and glowing, polished furniture, inlaid and embellished with ormolu.

The cumulative beauty of this left Jenny breathless and dizzy. She had never seen so many gorgeous things in one place.

They hovered, shoulder to shoulder, not quite touching, outside a succession of perfect window displays, pointing out to one another the particular treasures to be found inside. One glass specialist had as her central showpiece a small, piecrust-edged wine table on which were crammed dozens of tiny scent bottles, richly ornamented enamel, and glass, and silver, topped with amethysts and garnets, cut glass or carved lapis-lazuli. One bottle, barely an inch long, was particularly enchanting, in pale green opaque glass with a delicate art-nouveau design of russet and dark green trees fused into the glass.

"Oh, look at that one," Jenny said. "I don't think I've ever seen a prettier example."

"Which one is that?"

"The little green one, with the trees. Though they are all lovely."

"Hang on," he said, walking into the shop.

He exchanged words briefly with the woman who ran the shop, and brought out a handful of notes and change from his trouser pocket. The dealer picked up the green bottle from the display and began to wrap it carefully in sheets of tissue paper. Jenny gestured frantically through the window. David raised his eyebrows in enquiry. "No," she mouthed at him, through the glass. But he ignored her.

"David, you idiot. I didn't mean I wanted you to buy it," she said, as he came back out of the shop.

"Why not? You like it, don't you?"

"Yes, of course. But I can't take it."

"It's not from me," he said. "It's from your father. He rang me first thing this morning, and said particularly that if there was anything you wanted, I was to make sure you got it."

"He rang you? Why? To check up on me?" Jenny asked, sharply.

"To make sure that you'd arrived all right, and that we had made contact. He was worried — he'd heard about the flight being delayed. He'd been phoning the flat where I'm staying but I've been out a lot. I gave him your hotel number. He says he's going to give you a call some time and, meanwhile, don't forget about the spree. So this is part of it."

"But I don't want it. I don't need presents like that from him."

"Oh, for heaven's sake," David said, exasperated. "It's only a little scent bottle. It's no big deal. George could buy you the entire display and not miss the money, so why not just stick it in your bag and be grateful?"

"No. I told you. I don't want any presents. From you, or from my father."

She pushed the packet towards him. He stuck his hands into the pockets of his dark blue suit. "If you want it, keep it," he said, bluntly. "And if you don't want it, throw it away. Now, if you don't mind, I have to see about this bureau I told you about."

She followed him down the corridor, fuming. But if he wouldn't return the bottle, she supposed there was not much she could do except keep it. It *was* very pretty... but she didn't like the idea of George dispensing her trinkets from afar, with David Maine as his agent, as if a rush of presents and giving her 'a call some time' would make up for all the years of silence.

The shop where David took her was one of the largest in the building, occupying the same amount of space as three or four smaller units, on a corner of a corridor. The shop's owner welcomed him effusively by name, and they haggled good-naturedly over the bureau in question, an extremely decorative item of furniture with a parquetry herringbone inlay of different woods on a fruitwood base. There were ormolu leaf mounts at the corners and cabriole legs, slender and elegant. It was clearly very expensive indeed. Eventually, David handed over a wad of notes, signed a purchase document, made arrangements in his fluent French, presumably about having the bureau delivered, and they shook hands with mutual satisfaction.

"Phew. It's not often I spend that much money in one transaction," David said, coming out of the shop. "I think I need a coffee. How about you?"

"I'd love one. Do you buy many things there?"

"You have to be kidding. It's the

Paris equivalent of Bond Street. There's no way I can afford those prices. In point of fact, I'm more likely to be selling him things than buying them. But just occasionally I get a client back home in England who wants a particular piece that isn't easily available, like that bureau, or a genuine Savonnerie carpet, or a boulle table with an established provenance, and doesn't much care what the price is. I run a search service for antiques — if I haven't got it in stock I can usually track it down. The bureau's for a pop singer with a stately home in Sussex. The songs are terrible, and the singing is worse, but he's got a great taste in furniture!"

They found a quite square close by, and a patisserie and coffee shop with the usual round tables and plastic woven chairs outside. David ordered coffees and squares of pastry with glazed cherry topping, and told her about his buying activities in Paris.

"I don't find much worth buying for profit in the city itself; there's the occasional bargain among the dross in the Rue St. Paul, or one of the smaller shops outside the centre, but on the whole Paris is too over-priced for me. I drive round the provinces sometimes and stock up on the country furniture. Not that that's cheap, either, but there's a big demand for those rustic beds and chairs and wardrobes, like the English pine. But there *is* one place, in Passy, as a matter of fact, where I've been going for years. He occasionally sells me a few bits and pieces for a marginally less exorbitant sum than he charges the tourists. I could take you there, if you're interested."

It was a generous offer, Jenny recognised. Antique dealers do not lightly reveal their sources, particularly to someone with an interest in the trade. She glanced at her watch. It was nearly twelve o'clock, and she had arranged to meet Marcel at two-thirty. But the shop in Passy would be on the way back to the hotel so there should be no problem about keeping her appointment.

"Yes, please," she said. Then she remembered something else.

"How far is it from here to the Place Vendôme? I have to go there first, if possible, to my father's bank."

"It's a couple of stops down the Métro, near Concorde, or else we could walk down the Rue de Rivoli. It wouldn't take long."

They walked along the crowded pavement, with its stone colonnades shading the shop fronts crammed with goods to tempt the rich tourists. 'Duty free for export' read the signs in almost all the windows. Pavement artists offered small, detailed paintings of Paris scenes, in the naı:ve style, to passers-by. Racks outside the shops were loaded with posters and badges, T-shirts proclaiming 'I love Paris,' and models of the Eiffel Tower and floating scarves, labelled Lanvin, Cardin, Balmain. There was a wafting of exotic scents from the perfume shops and the muffled clink of china overhead from Smith's English Book Shop and Tea Rooms.

David turned right, leading her along the Rue Castiglione, past the pillared entrances to grand hotels, their names embossed in gold on the pavement underfoot, within circles of inlaid mosaic. The great, glazed doors opened to cool, luxurious entrance halls, and there were distant views of sunny courtyards with fountains and flowers. Uniformed doormen sprang forward in welcome as the very rich and very chic of the world swept up and down the steps, to and from the waiting limousines. It was a different world, Jenny thought, only a few hundred yards away from cafés and supermarkets and street stalls offering their cut-price clothes and all the impendimenta of everyday life.

The Place Vendôme was a great circle of creamy stone buildings spread around a soaring central monument like a spire. The square seemed relatively peaceful in the midday sun, away from the unceasing roar of traffic in the Rue de

Rivoli. There were the discreet doors of the Ritz and Van Cleef and Arpels, their names inscribed in gold on the windows — signs were out of place in this elegant double crescent, where commerce was a matter for gentlemen. To her dismay, when Jenny found the bank she had been looking for, there was a notice on the door to the effect that the foreign till would be closed from twelve noon until half-past two. It was ten-past twelve.

"Oh, no!" said Jenny.

"Is that so terrible? We can have lunch and come back later."

"I can't," Jenny explained. "I'm supposed to be meeting Marcel at two-thirty, for some shopping."

"Oh," he said bleakly. "I see. It *is* difficult, then. Do you need some money? I can let you have some? How much?"

"I don't really know. Quite a lot. I was going to see how much he had transferred for me — my father, that is. He said I could use it to buy some clothes."

"So he does have his uses," David said. "OK, OK, I'm sorry. Don't hit me. I never said a word." He raised his hands in mock-submission as she turned furiously on him, her face flaming at the implied criticism. "It's his business, and yours, what he gives you and how you take it. Do you want some cash or don't you? George said anything you wanted. I guess he meant anything in reason. How about ten thousand francs? Will that see you through till tomorrow? Or would you rather take twenty thousand?"

Ten thousand francs was more than nine hundred pounds. Jenny was shocked, both at the idea of his carrying so much money around with him, and at the notion that she might be expected to spend it in the course of one afternoon.

"It's far too much, of course," she protested.

"I wouldn't bet on that if you're going shopping with Marcel. He moves in classy circles — and he gets a commission in most of them," David added nastily. "So you won't be going home with a cheap scarf or two."

"I won't be buying anything I don't want to," Jenny told him. "Did you mean that, though, about the commission?"

"He gets it on what Angela buys," David said. "I don't know what he'll do with you."

"Does she know?"

"I expect so. Angie's no fool, especially when it comes to money. She must think he's worth it, in other ways."

"I dare say you're right," Jenny said meaningfully, thinking of gold cufflinks. Was it Angela's present he was wearing now, in the half-inch of pale blue shirt cuff visible below the sleeves of his impeccably styled midnight blue suit?

"You don't like Angela, do you?"

"I wouldn't know. I've only just met her. And she didn't say very much at the time: not to me, at any rate."

"She's not bad," he said. "She's a bit over the top sometimes. But she has a tough time."

"I'll take your word for it. It must be so difficult, living in that great big manor house, with all those tiresome servants, and all the boring, tedious money . . . darling."

"She pays for it other ways," David said quietly. "And she worked hard for it. OK, so things are easy now, for the time being. She's had one successful TV series and now, this minute, she's top of the media pops. But for twenty-five years before that she was a nobody in the acting profession, which is twenty-five years of kicks and rejections and taking just about any kind of work that came along in order to scrape a living. Now she's made it, and all she can think is: What happens if it all evaporates? What if I flop in the next rôle? What happens when the wrinkles take over? Sure, she's a poser. She has to be."

Jenny was jolted by the vehemence with which he defended Angela Torrance. Was he in love with her? It was not unknown for young men and older women to have such liaisons, and Angela, she had to admit, was a very sexy woman. She felt a sickening surge of jealousy.

"Bring on the violins," she snapped.

"I forgot," David said coldly. "You're not a very sympathetic person, are you? You don't give sympathy, and you don't take it. Here's the money. Do you still want to go with me to Passy, or do you want to grab a taxi and hurry back to get dolled up for a spending spree with Marcel?"

The morning had gone sour. 'Why do I have to keep arguing with him?' she asked herself wearily. 'He always seems to get to me and make me say the worst possible things.'

"I'll come with you," she said, "if that's all right. I don't need to get back until two-thirty, as I said. I'm meeting Marcel and Laurie at the hotel."

"Laurie?" he said, surprised.

"Yes, I asked Marcel to bring her along. She seemed a bit bored."

"I didn't even know you'd met her."

"Only very briefly, yesterday. But

Marcel told me about her. I gather she's left to her own devices, pretty much, while her governess is ill."

"It's good of you to bother," he commented. "I take it back about the sympathy, I guess."

"You don't have to," she said.

"Is that your favourite phrase?" he replied, with downright hostility.

The antique shop was in a dusty side street, unadorned by trees, or balconies or potted plants, which dropped downhill from the Avenue Mozart. The window had not been washed for weeks, and the sign was so faded as to be almost illegible, but inside it was so crowded with a mass of furniture and ornaments that David and Jenny had to edge their way gingerly along narrow gangways between chaotic piles of chairs and tables, and delicate, precariously poised knick-knacks, towards a dim little cubby hole of an office at the back of the shop. Some of the goods were shabby and neglected, some were downright junk, but a few items, Jenny's experienced eyes picked out, were quality goods, perhaps in need of polishing and repair, but potentially valuable.

A short, balding man appeared from the office, groping for the spectacles which hung from a chain round his neck. He was untidily dressed in shirtsleeves and ancient corduroy trousers, with a pair of battered plimsolls on his feet, but Jenny noticed that his watch was gold, and the signet ring on one of his fingers was a high-quality, expensive intaglio cameo. His cautiously polite welcome dissolved into a smile of genuine pleasure as he put on his spectacles and recognised one of his visitors. His gold teeth flashed as he shook David warmly by the hand.

"*Daveed! Quelle surprise! Mais tu es bienvenu, comme d'habitude!*"

"*Allo, Jules. Comment ça va?*"

The little Frenchman shrugged and spread his hands. "*Comme ci, comme ça . . . Bonjour, Mademoiselle.*" He turned to Jenny, took her hand and kissed it, with a flourish.

"This is Jules Severin, Jenny. An old friend."

"Ah, the lady is English!" said the dealer, with a thick accent. "Or American, perhaps?"

"English. Jenny Chatham, the daughter of another old friend."

"And you are showing 'er Paris?"

"That's right."

"It is a romantic city," said Jules, turning to Jenny with his hand spread extravagantly across his heart. "Ah, David, you are a lucky man to have a friend with a so-beautiful daughter."

"Sure," David said wryly. The dealer raised his eyebrows but did not comment. David was already looking about. "I'm after the usual things, Jules. Got anything to show me?"

"I have a few little pieces put aside," Jules said "In the back of the yard, if you will come through. Does the young lady wish to come as well, or would she prefer to stay in the shop?"

"I'll come, if I may," Jenny said.

"The 'back of the yard' was a small,

stone-built shed reached across a courtyard of cracked concrete, planted in the centre with a single, depressed-looking tree, but the contents were more up-market than the rest of Jules' stock. Jenny supposed that it was reserved for regular customers, and that local shoppers and tourists had to make do with the cheaper purchases in the main showroom. David made a rapid and expert selection, and looked over the interesting items for damage or woodworm, testing chairs, weighing them in his hands and pointing out defects. The two men bargained in friendly undertones.

Jenny stood by, estimating what the things might fetch if auctioned at Somerton's, and what they might be expected to sell for in an English antique shop. She made rough conversion calculations of some of the prices she overheard, and reckoned that David was indeed getting his purchases for a fair, if not a bargain price.

Her eye was caught by a chair, one of

several items David had initially put to one side then returned to the main group on hearing the price Jules quoted. It was a Louis Quinze armchair in fruitwood, with beautifully detailed, crisp carving on the arms, the curved fret of the back, and the strong cabriole legs. The upholstered seat was in a frayed and decayed state, with some of the stuffing missing, but that was easy enough to remedy.

She could see that the chair had been well cared for, and probably a torn top cover had been removed before it came into the storeroom, to reveal the more ragged undercover, because the actually woodwork was in good condition. Apart from a few shallow dents and gouges, coloured and disguised by years of polishing, there were no signs of damage. It was an extremely pretty chair, and Jenny's interest in it was increased by the fact that in her flat at home, she had another one, a family heirloom, which might have been its twin.

"How much is this chair, Jules?" she asked.

"Four thousand, five hundred francs, Mademoiselle. It is genuine of its period, and in good condition."

"Yes, I can see that. But it's a lot of money."

"I cannot sell for less, Mademoiselle. I think I could get more from a dealer who is coming in next week."

"Are you looking at the chair? It's pretty, isn't it? But too much money, Jules," said David.

The Frenchman shrugged. "I 'ave to make a living, David."

"Don't we all," David said, grinning. "I'll take the ones I've picked out, then, Jules, and I'll be along to pick them up on Friday or Saturday, if that's all right with you." He peeled off notes from what was by now a thinning wad, and pocketed his receipt. "Coming, Jenny? It's nearly twenty-past two."

Jenny gave the chair a last, longing glance. It was beautiful but she shouldn't even be considering it at that price. She was unemployed, after all, and there was the problem of getting a bulky piece of furniture home. "I'll have to think about it," she told Jules.

"Come *on*, Jenny," David said. "You don't want to keep Marcel waiting."

"No panic, he'll still be there," she said sweetly.

They arrived at the hotel nearly ten minutes late, and the electric blue Mercedes was parked in the square. Marcel and Laurie stood together, looking about for them. Laurie hurled herself towards them enthusiastically.

"Oh, hi, David. Are you coming too?" Marcel looked less than delighted to see him.

"Hello, David. We are going to the *Galleries de la Fontaine*. Not your scene, I think?"

"Hi, Laurie," David said, bending down to give the little girl a swift, affectionate hug. "No, I'm not coming, too. But I'll be along to the house later, so I'll see you then."

Laurie looked disappointed, but didn't

argue. She turned shyly to Jenny.

"Hi. I'm sorry I didn't say hello properly yesterday. Marcel says I must thank you for inviting me along."

"Hello, Laurie. No need to thank me. I'm going to buy a dress, so I need another woman's opinion," Jenny said. "And maybe I can do the same for you, if you'd like to look for a dress as well."

"I haven't any money."

"That's all right. I'll stand you one." 'All on George's money,' she thought, recklessly.

Laurie's eyes lit up. "Can I really choose something for myself? Usually Mom picks all my clothes." The dress she had on made that clear, Jenny thought. It was in bright splashes of scarlet and deep Mediterranean blue and gold on a vivid orange background. The kaftan shape was stylish in itself, but Laurie was a thin child with sallow skin and big dark eyes. Bright colours and bulky shapes simply didn't suit her.

"Certainly you can choose. Angela won't mind, will she?" Jenny said, a little apprehensively to Marcel.

"I doubt if she will notice," he replied carelessly.

They drove to the Champs-Elysées and parked in an underground car park, then travelled by escalator to the main street. Marcel led the way along the crowded pavement to a wide doorway, with the name of the arcade inset in gold letters over the arch. There seemed to be more tourists than native French people in this world famous street. The accents around them were English, American, German. Inside the cool, well-lit arcade, the shops were stocked with elegantly crafted leather shoes and handbags from Gucci or Kurt Geiger or Bally Suisse, and the dresses, draped with classic simplicity in the gleaming windows, were labelled with the names of top couture houses such as Balenciaga and Givenchy.

Jenny had not often studied such clothes, because they were outside her normal purchasing power, but she could see the perfection of detail that made them so desirable to those rich enough to afford them. There were very few price tags to be seen, and she was beginning to be apprehensive. She had taken David's ten thousand francs, with no intention of spending that much. But clearly, in these surroundings, ten thousand francs would not go very far.

"These clothes are too expensive for me," she said frankly to Marcel. He looked surprised.

"But I thought your father was paying?"

"Even so, I'm not in the market for these kinds of clothes."

"But the haute couture is an investment," Marcel protested.

"I prefer something less perishable, like antiques," Jenny told him.

He shrugged. "Not all the shops are so expensive here," he said. "There are the less well-known designers, too. And even at St. Laurent, you can buy a very nice evening dress, ready to wear, for a few hundred pounds." In his opinion, his voice implied, a few hundred pounds was cheap. Jenny wondered what his background was. A secretary's pay, even in the employment of a film and TV star, could not be all that high, but Marcel dressed, and spoke, and generally looked more like a jet-setter than a secretary.

"Have you always done the same kind of work you are doing now?" she asked him.

"No," he said. "Until this year, I helped my father in his business. But, *malheureusement*, the business did not do well, and so this year my father is abroad, to start something else, and so I work for Angela. Also it is easy for me this way to look after the estate."

"The estate?" she asked.

"The house that Angela is living in belongs to my family," Marcel said simply, "as does the farmland surrounding it. My father is the Vicomte de Roseul."

'Someone might have told me,' Jenny thought. '*David* might have told me, to be specific.' He had said. "You're not in his league financially..." she remembered now. And had gone on to suggest that Marcel might encourage her to spend money in expensive shops where he had privately arranged a commission for introduction customers. The son of a vicomte? A 'down-at-heel vicomte,' David had called him, a man with a failed business....

Laurie had stopped at a window full of children's clothes, and was looking longingly at a navy blue dress with a white collar which was displayed on a model. It was utterly plain, beautifully cut, and would suit her perfectly, Jenny noted.

"Do you like that dress?"

"Gee, yes," Laurie breathed. "The shape is so pretty. And I like the way the lines go." The only decoration was a top-stitched seam detail. It was unusual for a young child to respond to so simple a style. Laurie had clearly been born with inherent dress sense. "Let's go in," Jenny said.

They bought the dreess, and Laurie emerged with a huge paper carrier on her arm, walking on air. She looked much less sallow when she was happy. Marcel, meanwhile, was looking a little restive.

"We have only an hour left before I must collect Angela from her coiffeur, and you have not yet found a dress for tonight."

"Sorry," Jenny said. "What do you suggest?"

They travelled down an escalator to a lower ground floor, and Marcel led the way to a small corner shop. The dresses on the racks were few, but all of them were in luxurious fabrics. The vendeuse seemed to know Marcel — which seemed to confirm David's comments about commission. Perhaps Angela shopped here often, and the acquaintance with the vendeuse was entirely because of that? Jenny told herself. She was about to examine the racks herself, as she would have expected to do in any of the English shops where she bought clothes. But the saleswoman examined her with an experienced eye.

"Size twelve, no?" she pronounced with decision.

"That's right," Jenny said.
"*Et l'occasion?*"
"Soirée," Marcel said.

The woman preceded them to a rack hung with evening gowns, from which she swept several dresses and draped them over her arm. Before Jenny could make any kind of choice, she had stalked off on her slender high heels towards the changing room. Jenny followed meekly while Laurie and Marcel sat down on spindly gold chairs in the showroom and prepared to pass judgment.

Jenny had to admit that the selected gowns were breathtaking. The first was an olive green chiffon, falling in layers from a draped cowl neckline at the front and a dramatically plunging back. The colour suited her green eyes and the auburn gleam of her hair, but she felt uncomfortable with the folds of fabric swathing her neck and breasts, and she was distinctively apprehensive about the back. It felt as though any careless movement would result in the entire dress falling off her shoulders and down to her waist. She shook her head. The vendeuse seemed in agreement.

"*Non, c'est pas bon pour vous.* It is not in your style," the girl said. She lifted up another dress, with a cream gauze overblouse, hand-painted in a swirl of exotic, pale butterflies, over a plain cream silk sheath which was slashed from the thigh to the hem. Jenny thought the fabric was beautiful, but she wasn't sure about the slashed skirt. Her last evening dress, bought three years ago for a university May Ball, had been a high-necked, long-sleeved, medieval style bought from a Oxfam shop. It was hard to imagine herself moving confidently in the glamorous clothes which she was trying on now.

The sales girl studied her critically. "*C'est possible,*" she pronounced. "We shall ask Monsieur."

Self-consciously, Jenny paraded in front of Laurie and Marcel. Laurie thought the dress was pretty, but Marcel was not entirely convinced. He went into a huddle with the vendeuse, explaining, gesticulating. She went back to the rack and showed him a black gown in heavy satin, very plain. He nodded. "*Oui, c'est mieux*," he said, and to Jenny, "Try this one."

"I don't usually wear black," she said doubtfully.

"Do you want to look as you usually do? Try it," he said.

The dress had its own built-in underslip, and too low cut to wear a bra. Jenny slipped it on, and the salesgirl zipped up the fastening at the back, giving her a little push towards the long mirror. "*Mais, c'est parfait, Mademoiselle.*"

It was a transformation. The style was absolutely simple, the shape of the bodice like that of a slip or nightdress, except for the luxurious weight of the satin. There was a spray of lilies, also in black, appliquéd from the right hip curving across the body to the left shoulder where it climbed above the bodice. The thin black shoulder straps crossed at the back, and the only touch of colour was a gold clasp holding the right hand strap to the dress. The fabric was so cleverly cut, on the bias and with a minimum of seaming, that it draped gracefully whether she walked or stood still.

Jenny stared at the reflection in the mirror. She looked — there was no other word for it — she looked sexy. Her skin, even after the sun of the last three days, was creamy pale against the unrelieved black of the dress, and the red tints glowed in her dark auburn hair. Somehow she was slimmer and more graceful, more curvy and more sophisticated in this dress than she could have imagined. And more beautiful. She walked out into the main room the fabric swaying smoothly from her thighs, catching the light on its smooth surfaces. She even walked differently in it. Marcel and Laurie burst into applause.

"*C'est magnifique*," Marcel said, simply, spreading his hands.

"Golly, gee, Jenny. You look like a film star," said Laurie.

Luckily, the dress wasn't totally beyond her means, although it was probably the only time in her life, Jenny thought, that she would spend this much on one garment.

She felt a little breathless. "My hairstyle doesn't seem quite right," she mentioned timidly.

"It is not," Marcel agreed. "But we will take care of that. I will ask Angela's hairdresser to create you something special and, while it is drying, the beautician can give you a full *maquillage*. I can phone from here."

He commandeered the telephone and, a few minutes later, Jenny heard herself being described, in voluble French, as a beauty in distress, in desperate need of the magic of Raymond's scissors. Marcel put the phone down with satisfaction.

"*Voilà*. It is all arranged." He smiled at Jenny. "I feel like the godmother in the fairy story by Perrault. Cinderella, you shall go to the ball."

6

IN Jenny's experience, hairdressers said to you, "How much do you want off today, dear?" and "Would you like to look at the style book, love?" Raymond was an artist, and would no more have dreamed of asking Jenny's opinion than he would have contemplated consulting a blank canvas. He sat her down, turned her head this way and that, and picked up strands of her hair, letting it slip through his fingers. He sighed heavily over its condition, the standard of the previous cut, and the lack of time given to him for the working of a miracle. When she had been thoroughly demoralised, he asked to see the dress for which the creation was required. Then he closed his eyes, sketched a few shapes lightly in the air with his scissors, opened his eyes again and advanced on Jenny. Next moment, to her trepidation, swathes of hair were falling on the floor all around her.

"I don't want it too short," she murmured. He ignored her. She crossed her fingers and hoped that the end result would not be too drastic.

Marcel had taken Laurie and Angela home, having arranged with Jenny that she should take a taxi back to her hotel and he would collect her there for the evening at eight o'clock.

When she had been shampooed, and curlered, and dried, and the new style had been coaxed into shape by Raymond's deft fingers, she was a little shy about going out into the daylight. It took some getting used to, this new, thick, elegant head of hair. Raymond had layered her long bob so that it swept back in curving wings from her forehead and over her ears, adding new drama to the bones of her face.

Raymond's salon had a jewellery department, from which he had produced a pair of long drop earrings in the shape of lilies, and a matching necklet, like a thin golden collar fastening at the base of her throat with a clasp made of two lilies entwined. Meanwhile, the make-up girl had applied cleansers and aromatic facial packs and toners, had shaped her brows into moulded arches and painted her nails, and then proceeded to add glow and definition and colour to her face with what seemed like dozens of small pots and brushes.

Jenny walked down the Champs-Elysées, in her ordinary cotton dress, but with a bag from the boutique of Nina de St. Cyr on her arm, and a hairstyle by Raymond swinging as she walked. She was gratifyingly aware of turned heads and admiring glances.

When Marcel collected her that evening, he was fluent in his praise.

"*Mais, c'est un transformation!* Jenny, you will drive every woman at this party wild with envy."

The Rue de Monceau was broad and straight, with sober stone façades broken by barred windows and big, double oak doors. But beyond the oak doors there were paved, flowery courtyards, and beyond one such courtyard was the house which Hank Henderson, movie producer, had hired for the summer.

Inside the marbled entrance hall, the floor inlaid with a Greek key pattern of contrasting marble, the guests handed over their coats and wraps before mounting the soaring curved stone stairway, with its black and gold bannister wreathed with flowers in delicate ironwork, to the main reception rooms. Here there were chandeliers blazing, and music playing — the music, a kind of orchestral pop seeming at odds with the surroundings — and what seemed to be literally hundreds of guests, gossiping and gyrating and greeting one another with cries of rapturous recognition.

Marcel seemed to know many of the guests, and Jenny was introduced in rapid succession to a bewildering number of strangers. But there was no denying that, in that dress, with her new, heightened looks, she was ready for this exalted company. She saw admiration, and speculation, in the eyes of the men, and frank or grudging acknowledgement that she was beautiful in the eyes of the women. She let it go to her head just a little, and there was a sparkle in her eyes which was not entirely due to the champagne she had drunk, or to the subtle shades of green blended into her eyelids by the beautician. Her walk had a spring to it which was only partly the effect of the black dress' flaring hem. She laughed and flirted, and turned her stylish head with conscious elegance, catching the sight of her stunning reflection in a whole series of ornate, gilt-framed mirrors set around the room.

Marcel left her to go in search of more champagne, leaving her in the company of a middle-aged American whose name she had failed to catch. He promptly told her, with a damp hand on her black satin hip, that she ought to be in the movies. Why didn't she come to see him tomorrow? He could fix her a screen test.

"I'm not an actress," Jenny said, disliking the sensation of his hand which was showing a disconcerting tendency to snake round to her bottom.

"No need to be," the man said. "It doesn't matter in the movies. You just have to be yourself."

"No, thanks," Jenny said, moving hastily away.

He sidled after her. "What a waste. With looks like yours, honey, you'd be a big star in no time. I mean it."

"No, really. I'm not interested." Jenny evaded his groping hand and, in doing so, bumped into a dinner-jacketed shoulder, which proved, when the man turned, to belong to David.

He had clearly heard every word of the exchange. "She means it," he said tersely to the discomforted lecher. "So leave her alone, will you?" The man moved away, after taking stock of David's height and determined manner.

"You've got more sense than I gave you credit for," David said. "That casting couch routine is as old as the hills, but the girls still fall for it." He looked her up and down, taking in her altered appearance. "Mind you, I can't blame the guy for trying ... You look like you're auditioning for Curse of the Vampires in that get-up. When's the funeral?"

Gratitude at being rescued from the adventurous hands of the unknown American dissolved. Jenny had hoped to make an impact on David with her new looks. She had imagined his reaction, as she put on the dress back at her hotel, imagined his eyes widening with stunned admiration, or even blatant desire. She had been half-looking for him ever since she had arrived, waiting for the moment when she would stand in front of him and he would draw that long, startled breath and say "Jenny? I never knew you could look like this ... " What a hope! He merely looked amused.

"As soon as you drop dead," Jenny said between her teeth.

"Nice one," he acknowledged unconcernedly. "Do you bite as well, or do you merely snap?"

Jenny drew a deep breath. "Why are you so rude to me?" she enquired tightly.

"Because I like watching you fizz, I guess." That did it, the words, and the inflection of his voice, sending her heartbeat hammering into overdrive and her stomach fluttering. Drat the man, it was too entirely easy for him to throw her off-balance. She held her head up, meeting his blue gaze squarely. The grin faded from his face. "Jenny," he said.

"Yes?"

"We have to get something straight."

It was at precisely that moment that Marcel returned with two brimming, bubbling glasses of champagne. "Here you are, *ma belle*," he said, ignoring David's hostile expression. "*Eh bien*, David, what do you think of the beautiful Cinderella? Quite a transformation, no?"

"Fine," David said, "if you like black widow spiders. I thought she looked all right before."

There was tension in the air between him and Marcel. They faced one another, with Jenny an almost irrelevant spectator, for a moment. Then Marcel said, gently, "You are in a bad mood, David. Didn't you have a good afternoon with Maxine? Oh, by the way, Angela is in the supper room, and she is just a little emotional ... I think she is looking for you."

David said something under his breath, and Marcel clicked his tongue reprovingly.

"Remember, David. She who pays the piper ... "

David stalked away in the direction of the supper room without a word.

"Who's Maxine?" Jenny asked, when he had gone. She hated herself for being weak enough to ask.

"One of David's ... er ... business acquaintances. A very attractive woman. How did you get on with Hank Henderson?"

"That man, the one with the roving hands? *He* was Hank Henderson? The man who's giving this party?"

"Yes. I introduced you."

"I didn't hear you properly. Oh, help," Jenny said. "He offered me a screen test, and I thought he was making a pass at me, and told him to get lost, more or less."

"He probably was making a pass at you," Marcel reassured her lightly. "And I wouldn't worry. He does it to all the girls. All the beautiful ones, anyway. He doesn't even remember which ones turned him down by the end of the evening. But you know," Marcel added thoughtfully, "it might be worthwhile if I have a little talk with him tomorrow, when he is sober, and remind him about the screen test. You have a good figure, and a very pretty face a voice with interesting timbre ... Who knows, you may be a star in the making?"

"You're joking," Jenny said, laughing.

"No, I am perfectly serious."

"Then you ought to be joking. I am not the least bit suited to being an actress."

"A pity," he said. "I could work for you instead of Angela. I would be your agent, and you could earn me lots and lots of money!"

"Don't you like working for Angela?" she asked.

"She drinks too much," he said, suddenly serious. "And when she drinks, she is either very unreasonable, or very . . . affectionate. I am not sure which is worse. But tonight, I do not have to worry," he added, smiling again, his tone becoming lighter. "It is David who has to worry."

Jenny wanted to ask more about David and Angela, David and Maxine, but she felt that however charming Marcel might be, he was not likely to stand for it if she tried to use him as a means of gaining information about another man, particularly one he didn't like. There was clearly no love lost between David and Marcel.

She tried to put her father's enigmatic, infuriating friend out of her mind. He had spent the afternoon with someone called Maxine, 'a very attractive woman.'

She drank some more champagne, and danced with Marcel, and stood smiling while he talked in rapid French to various friends and they made awkward conversation with her in English far less fluent than Marcel's. Sometimes they made remarks to him which she managed to discern were about her, and which, if crude, were complimentary. Time passed. At midnight, everyone who was still there, which meant most of the company, flowed into the supper room and helped themselves to a sumptuous buffet which had been laid out on thirty feet of catering table swathed in snowy linen.

Jenny, who wasn't used to champagne and was at the stage of enunciating her vowels carefully, was grateful for the break. She had been dancing with Marcel and the music had got progressively slower and more atmospheric, and the couples who danced had got more and more intimately entwined as they moved around the polished parquet. Marcel had been holding her very close, which was a pleasant sensation in itself, very different from her tense few minutes in David Maine's arms the previous night, and she had glanced up over his shoulder at one stage and seen David, halfway across the room, with Angela Torrance draped like the Ancient Mariner's albatross around his neck and his eyes fixed on Jenny. She had become suddenly aware that Marcel's hands were travelling sensuously across her back, something she had hardly noticed as an individual sensation until that moment, and that, judging by the look on David's face he minded.

She was too hazy to make any sense of it. But she pushed herself gently away from Marcel, and said, searching for an excuse, "I'm starving."

So the supper came at a fortunate moment.

Apart from the long tables which were spread with food, behind which a staff of professional caterers were poised to help the guests to their choice of food, the supper room held a number of small tables, seating six or eight people, at which the diners could group themselves. Marcel had thoughtfully teamed up with a mixed party of French and American friends, so that she would not feel left out of the conversation, and she was being entertained by a long involved and helplessly funny account of a disastrous skiing trip by a small, snub-nosed American girl and her crop-haired boy friend — who, she gathered, was a script writer on Hank Henderson's next project — when there was a disturbance at the other end of the room: a splintering of glass, and a crash, as a plate hit the floor, and a woman's voice, high and strident, ranting about her companions, the "lousy, two-faced, money-grubbing swines," and how they were trying to trick something out of her, and how she was surrounded by parasites . . .

A man's voice, low and steady, interrupted her, repeating soothing phrases, but the woman railed against him, breaking out into new torrents of invenctive.

Across the dimly-lit room, Jenny saw a bronzed back, a dress in scarlet and purple gauze, a mane of wildly disordered blonde hair, and beyond her, David, his face expressionless, quietly reasoning.

"Oh, *mon Dieu*," Marcel muttered to himself. "*Elle commence encore.*" He put his hands to his face, covering his aquiline nose in a resigned gesture. "It's Angela," he said unnecessarily to Jenny. "I had better go and see what I can do."

Jenny followed him down the room. Angela had cleared a space for herself. Apart from David, the rest of the guests at her table had retreated to a safe distance. There was a large red wine stain on the white tablecloth and a scattering of broken glass on the floor at her feet. A further target for the wine had clearly been David, judging by the stains spreading across his dinner jacket and shirt, which he was disregarding. Angela had by now stopped shouting, and was sobbing uncontrollably into her hands, her eyes closed and her face contorted. Mascara and glittering eyeshadow ran in streaks down her cheeks.

"All you're interested in is the darned money," she sobbed. "Don't try to kid me. You're no better than any of them. You know everything about me, things I never even told my mother, and you'll use it against me in the end. They always do."

"That's not true," David said quietly.

"You don't give a damn about me," Angela wept. The guests watched, fascinated. David ignored them. A flashlight bulb popped, and then another.

"Now it will be in the papers," Marcel muttered.

"You undervalue yourself Angie," David was saying. "You don't give yourself a chance. Sure, I care about you. So do a lot of other people. You have to rate yourself higher." His hand was on her shoulder. The words were soothing and repetitive.

"How can I do that? I make a mess of everything I touch. I'm a lousy actress and a lousy wife and mother. Laurie's afraid of me. Mike hates me."

"No, he doesn't," David said steadily. "He cares about you. So does Laurie. Just give it a chance. Don't go making people run away from you, Angie..."

Suddenly she stood up, stumbled, and clung to him with her face pressed against his wine-stained jacket. Another little flurry of flashlights went up from a different part of the room.

"Take me home," she whispered. His arm encircled her supportively.

"All right," he said, gently his hand stroking her dishevelled hair. He looked over her shoulder and saw Marcel and Jenny hovering. At that, Marcel moved forward. "Do you need any help?"

David looked strained. "No, it's OK," he said. "I'll take her home now. She's pretty tired. How's it going, Jenny?"

"All right," she said stiffly. He gave her a brief smile and then someone brought Angela's coat and someone else started to sweep up the broken glass. There was the murmur of conversation restarting around the room and the incident was over.

Suddenly Jenny herself felt deathly tired. It was she realised, one o'clock in the morning. At home in England it would be two a.m. The champagne exhilaration had worn off and she had the beginnings of a pounding headache between her eyes. "I'd like to go home now, as well, if that's all right with you," she told Marcel.

"Certainly, *chérie* My place or yours?" She glanced up at him, startled, but it had been a joke because he went on, seriously, "I hope this hotel of yours has a night porter. I forgot to check before we left. Did you?"

Marcel fetched the lacy shawl which she had bought that afternoon on her way home from Raymond's salon and wrapped it solicitously round her. In the car, she drifted lightly into sleep and woke as the Mercedes pulled into the side of the road in front of the hotel. The Mercedes, it seemed, belonged to Marcel and not to Angela, as she had originally assumed. Angela must have gone back to her stucco manor house in David Main's borrowed silver grey Lotus. It alarmed Jenny how much that realisation bothered her. David was taking up far too much of her thought processes for comfort.

Marcel switched off the engine, and she saw his bony, aquiline profile clearly defined against the light of a street lamp. He turned towards her. Jenny knew perfectly well that he was going to kiss her, but was totally undecided as to what her reactions to such an event might be. While she was still trying to make up her mind, it happened.

He tasted of wine, she noticed, first of all. He had a dry, soft mouth, and his approach was reassuringly experienced and efficient, with no bumping of noses or awkward preliminary grapplings. His hands, when they took hold of her, did so firmly, and when they moved they moved into the right places, so that she was supported and caressed. The problem from Jenny's point of view was that the whole embrace seemed for her to be totally devoid of emotional involvement, as if it was happening, not to her, but to someone else.

She climbed out of the car, weak with relief that is was over, and he walked with her up the shallow flight of steps to where the hotel door, under its dim overhead light, was firmly closed.

Marcel tried the handle. "It is locked," he told her.

"Oh, help." Jenny was remembering a notice on the back of the door in her room which asked the guests, if they intended to get back after midnight, to ask for a key. She looked up helplessly at the façade, with its rows of darkened windows. There was no sound from the interior of the building. Marcel rang the bell, and they heard it buzzing loudly by the reception desk. There was a pause. He rang again. At last a light came on behind the door and, after an interminable three or four minutes, there was the sound of a key turning in the lock.

Madame Lafayette was not amused. Awful in her dressing-gown, she drew herself up, and although at least six inches shorter than Jenny, she was intimidating in her indignation.

"*Mademoiselle. si vous aurez tard, autrefois, prière de demander un clef avant de sortir.*"

Jenny stammered awkward apologies and excuses to the effect that she had forgotten to ask for the key, that she hadn't realised she would be so late, that she was terribly sorry to disturb Madame, and in the course of all this, was swept inside, and the door was firmly closed upon Marcel. When Jenny reached her room, still abjectly apologising, and Madam Lafayette had at last stalked away, she looked out of the window into the square, and saw that Marcel was standing by his blue Mercedes. He looked up, saw her at the window, and waved a hand in salute before driving away.

He was a dear, she thought. So kind and considerate and gentle. How ridiculous that David Maine had called him a 'Gallic Romeo'. He could certainly teach David a thing or two when it came to manners . . . It was ironic, and unsettling, that Marcel, despite his *savoir faire* and his courtesy, should be so resistible, while David, who was a smug, critical, impatient, conceited oaf — she listed his defects bitterly — could send her pulse rate up with just one of those thoughtful blue glances... when he wasn't stoking her temper to boiling point with his casual insults! She fell asleep, blurredly determined not to think about the man any more, but his face slipped insistently into her dreams.

7

THERE was a knock at the door. Jenny heard it through a fog of sleep. Her subconscious mind tried to absorb it into a dream, failed, and she was jolted into consciousness. She rolled over and groped for her watch: eight o'clock. Breakfast was early — she had ordered it for eight-thirty, having got back so late last night, for which she was probably still highly unpopular. She sat up in bed and pushed her disordered hair out of her eyes. The flowing waves of Raymond's inspired creation must look a mess by now.

The knocking was repeated. The door was not locked; she had left it unlatched for the chambermaid. "*Entrez*," she called. But instead of a cheerful Frenchwoman with a tray, it was David Maine who walked into the room.

Jenny snatched the sheet up to her

chin and subsided under the bedclothes, acutely conscious of her revealing nightdress. A moment later she realised that, after all, he had seen more of her in a bikini by Angela's pool than was currently on show. She felt doubly embarrassed by the gauche gesture.

David merely raised his eyebrows. "Did I wake you up? Sorry. I'm on my way somewhere and wanted a quick word with you first. Do you need this?" He unhooked her negligée from behind the door and tossed it to her, and she struggled into it, feeling distinctly at a disadvantage.

"First of all," David said, "I have a note to deliver." He advanced into the room, bringing an envelope out from the pocket of one of his seemingly inexhaustible supply of well-cut suits. He waited politely for her to read the contents. It was from Marcel: "*I am sorry that I cannot keep our appointment this morning.*" She vaguely remembered arranging to go to the *Musée de Cluny*, and was relieved that she would not have to do so. From what she could remember of her conduct last night, meeting Marcel again was going to be an awkward experience. She read the rest of the note. *"I have to work, Angela needs me all day, but please have supper with me tonight instead. If this is not possible, ring me — "* there was a phone number printed across the head of the paper — *"otherwise I shall collect you at half-past eight. Je t'embrace. Marcel."*

"You will have gathered," David said, watching her, "that he's tied up for the rest of the day. If that's bad news, my commiserations."

"When did he give you this?"

"First thing this morning, at breakfast. I stayed the night at Angie's." David said briefly.

"Oh. How is Angela?"

"A bit subdued, chiefly due to a monumental hangover. She's swearing to go on the wagon and reorganise her life, and has decided to start by reading all the scripts that have been awaiting her attention for the past three months.

Hence Marcel's call to duty; he will have to write all the polite rejection notes. And if you want to know how Marcel is, he's fine. Boring the pants off us all at breakfast by reciting the list of your virtues. He says you are beautiful, warm, witty and modest, among other things. Clearly, you have hidden depths."

"Thank you so much," Jenny said. "Did you wake me up to tell me this?"

"No, it's an extra. I came to say, if you want to go to Versailles today I can take you. But it would have to be between twelve-thirty and five o'clock, because I have an appointment for this morning and one for early evening.

"Well, if you're that busy again — " Jenny began.

"There's no need, and I don't have to. I know. Same old song. I made the appointments because I thought you'd be occupied with Marcel. You seem to be his favourite hobby currently. It's a bit difficult to cancel them now. But, like I said, I'm free between twelve-thirty and five. Do you want a lift to Versailles or not?"

"All right. Fine." Jenny shrugged her shoulders. "But I can't think why you should bother."

"I promised George," he said expressionlessly.

"I'm sure he'll be touched to hear how nobly you're keeping your word," Jenny murmured.

David scowled. "Now, look," he began, then changed his mind. "Aw, forget it, I'll pick you up at twelve-thirty."

Jenny spent a hectic morning in the Boulevard Hausseman, looking for a dress to wear to Versailles. Not that she cared what David thought about her appearance, of course, but she would feel better able to hold her own against that self-contained young man if she looked halfway decent. Her demure cotton dresses seemed even more dowdy with the new hairstyle, and George *had* told her to buy whatever she needed.

But with two new dresses and a pair of shoes in carrier bags on her arm, she was suddenly assailed by the pangs of conscience. She had not intended to spend all the money that David had advanced her on the previous day, but it was almost gone. She remembered the overtones of criticism in his voice as he had said, 'So he does have his uses'. She had made it clear that she felt no great affection for George, her absentee father, but she had been ready to pocket the presents which he probably thought were an adequate compensation for the past. But she was not prepared to be bought off, she decided. Let George live with his conscience, if he had one, about leaving his wife and daughter. She could pay for her own clothes.

She found a Paris branch of her own bank, near the Gare St. Lazaire, and after some delay and a long-distance phone call to her branch at home in Ashfield, she was able to withdraw enough in francs to pay David back what he had lent her the previous day. She tried not to think of the hole it would make in her bank account, or of her jobless state.

A coffee in a bar-tabac and a quick trip round the *Jeu de Paume* gallery lifted her spirits. She sat in the Tuileries gardens and fed crumbs from the pastry of a melting *tarte aux framboises* to a couple of ingratiating pigeons, and then it was time to go back to the hotel and get ready to meet David.

The new dress she had chosen was a confidence booster, in a finely-pleated linen fabric, sleeveless and elegant. The bodice, edged in bronze to contrast with the natural linen colouring, crossed over at the front and fastened at the waist. She had chosen bronze sandals, with slender high heels and an ankle strap, which seemed to emphasise the length of her long, bare legs, and a shoulder bag in squashy, soft leather into which she crammed her passport, purse and the wad of francs with which she intended to repay David

As she brushed out her shining hair and sprayed herself with scent, the girl in the mirror seemed as unfamiliar as the glamorous creature of the previous night. It wasn't just the smart new clothes, or the sophisticated hairstyle, or even the proud, new tilt of her chin. There was something else: a sort of breathless expectancy about her which Jenny Chatham, long-time fiancé of Piers Somerton, had somehow lacked. Bright eyes and glowing cheeks . . . Paris fever, she told herself, and hummed the cabaret song as she ran downstairs.

David was late. It was nearly one o'clock when he finally arrived. The new dress, naturally, was entirely wasted on him.

"Sorry I'm so late," he called, opening the passenger door of the Lotus. "We got talking and I forgot the time."

"We?"

"Claudie's an old customer. And a friend. Let's go, shall we, or there won't be enough time."

She sat in the silver grey Lotus, resenting his indifference.

"I had an early lunch," he told her — with Claudie, whoever she might be, presumably. "There's a salad baguette and some fruit in a bag on the back ledge. Will that do for you, or do you want to stop off somewhere? We really don't have too much time."

"It's really good of you to fit me in like this," Jenny said, between her teeth.

"Yes, isn't it?" he replied imperturbably.

Versailles was crammed with tourists, although the season was not yet at its height.

"It's always crowded," David said. "If it isn't the tourists, it's the school parties getting an eyeful of their heritage. You have to queue for everything. We'd better park in one of the side streets near the main avenue." He drove round, irritated by the lack of parking spaces, while Jenny tried to imagine the area before the days of tarmacadam streets and cars and coach parties, when the long buildings lining the avenue were still the Royal Mews, housing the horses of the Sun King's vast and sprawling retinue of servants and courtiers. Eventually they found a space, and as they were getting out of the car, Jenny remembered the money in her bag which she did not want to carry round the palace with her in case of pickpockets.

"Before we go, can I give you back that money you lent me yesterday?" She opened her bag.

"So you managed to get back to the Place Vendôme, did you?"

"No, this is from my bank," she said. "I won't be using George's money."

"Why not? Didn't you say he transferred it for your use, specially?"

"I just don't want to, that's all. I'd rather buy my own things."

"Is it because of something I said?" he demanded.

"No. Why on earth should it be?"

"Because you seemed ready enough to spend it yesterday morning."

When she didn't reply, he continued, "I don't know why you have to make such a big fuss about a few clothes from your father . . . When he phoned me, he sounded really keen for you to have a good time. Why hurt his feelings by turning it down? Why not just buy the clothes, or whatever, and thank him nicely, like anyone else would?"

"Because," Jenny said, coldly, "I want a father, not a credit card."

"Well, have you let him know just what, in your estimation, adds up to a father? My guess is, he doesn't know how to go about it; after all, you're practically a stranger to him, aren't you?"

"That's hardly my fault. If he'd stuck around, I wouldn't be."

"It's too late to do anything about that. But now he wants to get to know you, and make up for things as best he can, why don't you give him a bit of help instead of wallowing in resentment?"

Jenny gave an exaggerated sigh and looked pointedly at her watch. "I thought we were in a hurry," she said. "Here's your money, do you want to check that it's all there?"

He threw it uncounted into the glove compartment. "Can I leave my bag in there as well?" Jenny asked. "Then I won't have to queue up to put it into the *consigne*." At some of the museums and galleries, large bags were not allowed to be carried around, as a precaution against vandals and thieves.

They went through the double gateway into the vast brick-paved courtyard in front of the palace, the grey bricks glaring almost white in the hot sun. The queues were discouragingly long, at every point of entry to the various attractions. "Heck," David said, "Every time I come here I say, 'Never again'. What exactly do you have to find out?"

Jenny produced George's list of details. She was shamed by how little of it she had tackled; this was her fourth day in Paris. David studied the list without enthusiasm. "It's crazy," he said. "There's nothing here he couldn't have got out of the average guide book."

"Maybe he hasn't got the average guide book."

"I could have sent one over. You can buy them anywhere in Paris. Why send you? It was the same with the list for the *Musé de la Marine.*"

"It is not my fault," Jenny said acidly, "if the list is not as exacting as you'd like it to be. It's the list George gave me, and I'm merely trying to supply the information as requested. Can we get on with it?"

The queue for the State Rooms stretched all the way across the courtyard. It was getting hot, and there was a perpetual noise of multilingual chatter from the waiting tourists. They stood for several minutes and the tail of the queue hardly moved at all. "This is ridiculous," David muttered. "We'll be here all day. For Pete's sake, why not just get a guide book?"

"I know you've seen it all before, and the greatest palace in the world inspires nothing more in you than a sense of *déjà vu,*" Jenny said. "But *I* am that despicable thing, a first-time tourist, and I happen to want to see it." She spoke particularly sharply because her feet, in the smart new sandals, were hurting already. She shifted her stance slightly, and his sharp eyes caught the movement.

"Oh, come on," he said. "You can't be serious about wanting to spend two hours standing under the hot sun in those shoes. You have to be crazy to be wearing new shoes to go sight-seeing, anyway. Tourist shoes should be old, flat and comfortable."

"Why not write a book about how to be a tourist?" Jenny suggested. "And then sell it to someone who wants your advice."

The queue moved forward a few steps, with collective patience. "Oh, to hell with this," David said. "If you like it, you do it. I'm going to wait in the garden. I'll see you by the steps at the head of the long avenue." When she looked bewildered, he added, "Ask a guide for the Royal Avenue and the Fountain of Latona. But don't forget I have to leave by five."

"I won't forget. I should hate to keep one of your lady friends waiting. Is it Claudie, or Angela?"

"Maxine, as a matter of fact. Well, so long. Have fun."

At a quarter to five, she emerged from the palace with a throbbing head, a nagging pain in her lower back, and a feeling that her stylish new shoes were several sizes too small. She had finally bought a guide book, and was grateful for its help in locating the Fountain of Latona among the extensive gardens which stretched away from the west front of the château.

It was a relief to get away from the noise and heat of the interior, and she was punch drunk with the number of exquisite works of art she had seen during the course of the last two and a half hours.

Even for someone like herself, for whom antiques had meant a career as well as an enthusiasm, the accumulated treasures of Versailles were too much to take in one dose. The Bourbons didn't merely refurnish or redecorate; when they tired of their surroundings or ran out of space they built another wing and carried on collecting. Jenny had dutifully looked out for the details George had asked for, but she was struck by the ease with which she had been able to obtain them. It was a little like filling in one of those questionnaires which school parties carry round to concentrate the children's minds. Real research, she had a feeling, should have taken her days, or even months, in a place like this. Would she have felt so doubtful of the value of what she was doing if David Maine hadn't been so scathing about it? She wasn't sure.

He had found a shady place under a tree, where the smoothly clipped lawns merged into woodland, and was stretched out, apparently asleep, with his head pillowed on his folded jacket. He had taken off his tie, unbuttoned his shirt at the neck, and rolled up his sleeves. One arm was tucked behind his head. Minus the effect of his sardonic grin and watchful blue eyes, he looked young and peaceful, and as usual, the sight of him did things to Jenny which the logical, independent female side of her resented. She felt keyed up and antagonistic as she knelt beside him,

"David." He didn't stir.

"David," she repeated, louder. She put out a cautious hand and touched his warm shoulder. He stirred and opened his eyes.

"Mmm?"

"I've seen what I needed."

"Jenny," he said, sitting up in one lithe movement. "What time is it?"

"A quarter to five. It's all right. You're not late."

"Thank heaven for that," he said.

"Would it matter so much? Is your punctuality all that vital?"

"Yes, it is, as a matter of fact. Maxine's a very rich lady, with a corresponding sense of her own importance." He checked with his own watch, and then relaxed. "I must have been more tired than I thought," he said. "Last night was somewhat fraught."

Last night, she recalled, he had been coping with a maudlin Angela Torrance.

He had taken her home from the party... and stayed the night. Well, it was no business of hers what that entailed.

"How did you get on?" he asked.

"All right," she said, flipping the well-filled pages of her notebook. "Do you mind if I sit down for a bit?"

"Tiring, isn't it, taking in the concentrated culture?"

"I'm exhausted,"! Jenny admitted, sinking on to the grass beside him and kicking off her shoes. "I think I'd have to come back dozens of times to take it all in."

"Count me out," he said lazily, lying down again.

"Naturally."

He propped himself on one elbow, looking up at her. "Boy," he said, lightly sarcastic. "You can really make a guy feel wanted, did you know?"

Jenny held his gaze. "Can I?" she asked. Her heart was thumping, suddenly, with echoing flutters in the region of her throat. David was a foot away from her and the conversation had cut without warning from banter to something serious, as it had done before: at the Pont D'Iena, at the pool, and for a moment at last night's party, when he had said, "We have to get something straight."

"You could," David said, deliberately. "If you wanted to. *Do* you want to?"

Jenny's eyes dropped. Like a coward, she shied away from the moment. It was somehow too important. "Depends on the guy," she said carelessly. "I think I got everything I was supposed to." She leafed through her notebook, trying to concentrate on the neat lineage of her notes.

"I shouldn't worry," David said pointedly. "It's all window-dressing, anyway."

"What do you mean?"

"My guess is, George doesn't need any of that stuff you're so zealously writing down in your little book. He has it already. It was just an excuse, to get you to take a holiday."

"That's ridiculous. Why should he have to invent spurious research?"

"Maybe he knew a sourpuss like you wouldn't just take a straightforward present. Maybe he knew he'd have to dress it up as work, or you'd be whining on about how there's no need, and he doesn't have to." His voice mimicked her English accent unkindly.

"Why should he?" Jenny said again. "Why be that eager to give me a holiday?"

"Because you're his daughter? Because the poor dumb fool is fond of you, or feels sorry for you? How should I know? But if what you've got in that notebook is research," David said, "then I'm John F. Kennedy. George always did have a soft heart," he added. "I suppose he'll eventually realise that it's thrown away on his darling daughter."

She didn't understand why he was so angry. Nor why she had the stupid urge to provoke him, except that when they weren't arguing, she felt so intensely vulnerable to his charm.

"George, *my father* George, is old

enough to make his own mind up about who he is, or isn't, fond of. It's nothing to do with you, anyway. Why don't you stay out of it? Or did he actually ask you to deliver me tedious little lectures on filial obedience and appreciation of his so-generous nature, along with chaperoning me round Paris? If he did, I wish he had kept his holiday!"

There was a short, highly charged silence. Then Jenny said, "Oh, for heaven's sake, don't let's snipe any more. It's just a waste of time, and it's too nice here." She lay back in the scented grass and closed her eyes, shutting out the sight of his exasperated, hostile expression. The sun was hot on her face, an orange glare behind her lids. There was a distant hum of voices and the splash of water in the fountains and the sound of a motor mower clipping the velvet lawns. She relaxed, stretching her arms out behind her head.

"I can't make you out," David's voice said, dangerously quite. "One minute you're sending me out 'come hither' signals like nobody's business, and the next you're telling me to get lost."

Jenny's eyes flew open. He was sitting beside her, so close that his head and shoulders blocked out the sun. There was a disturbing glint in his blue eyes.

"I don't know what you're talking about," she said, hastily trying to sit up. But his hand closed over her nearest wrist, pegging it to the ground.

"Don't you?" he said. "Then maybe it's time we got it clear." Her free hand jerked up to push him away, but ineffectually, because he caught it and forced it back, pinning her on the grass. He knelt above her, looking down, the weight of him holding her helpless, panting with indignation.

She couldn't get away.

She didn't want to get away.

She stopped struggling and lay passive, waiting for his next move which would surely be to kiss her as he had done two days ago in Angela Torrance's garden. The rapid beating of her heart seemed to be the only sound in the scented gardens of Versailles at that moment, and David Maine the only other human being in the world. He was breathing carefully, and the muscles of his jaw, neck and forearms were rigid with tension. She felt again an odd mixture of elation and fear at having succeeded in shaking him out of his more customary, casual élan.

Then abruptly, he released her and stood up, brushing the grass cuttings from his knees. Her first reaction was one of disappointment.

"That for instance, was one of your come hither moments."

Jenny scrambled to her feet, humiliated, her cheeks burning at the sudden switch from challenge to dismissal.

"How dare you manhandle me?" she cried.

"And that's the 'get lost' part that invariably follows. You're a tease, Jenny and it seems to me," David said tauntingly, "that you could do with a lot more manhandling, the way you behave. Some day, sweetheart, someone is going to dust your beautiful backside for you and teach you a lesson."

"Well, it won't be you, Mr. Maine!" She longed to erase the self-assurance from his arrogant face. Her fists itched to pummel him out of his damnable indifference.

"Don't count on it," he said pleasantly. "You might push your luck too far. Well, it's been a delightful experience talking to you, Miss Chatham, but I have to work, as I have no rich Daddy keen to underwrite *my* holiday expenses, so if you intend getting back to Paris in my car, you'll have to calm down and come along now." He scooped up his jacket and started to walk away from her.

"I'd rather take the train," Jenny flung after him.

"Please yourself," he retorted, not turning round.

She watched his lean, athletic figure striding briskly away and tried to cool her furious feelings. Drat the man, he always brought out the worst in her! No one else had ever made her so edgy, so sensitive to nuance and undercurrent. Every lazy, barbed word set her nerves tingling, and she was ready to flare up at the merest hint of an insult.

The worst of it was he was so undeniably attractive. Even while part of her was hating him, another part was fascinated by his looks and his voice and his casual, co-ordinated efficiency. Of which, no doubt, he was very well aware.

He was out of sight beyond the archway which led past the ticket and souvenir bureau towards the main courtyard, when Jenny suddenly realised that her handbag was locked in the glove compartment of his car. Without it, she had no money for a train ticket back to Paris.

"Oh, *no!*" she muttered ferociously. It was the last straw . . . but it wasn't, because as she ran over the cobbled paving of the huge open courtyard between the palace and the main gate, she stumbled, twisting her ankle sideways. With a sharp crack, the heel broke off her new shoe.

Jenny could have cried. But that wouldn't

do much good. She gritted her teeth and took off both shoes, limping painfully on, barefoot. At least her ankle, though wrenched, had not been sprained and she could still walk. But the chances that David's car would be still be where they had left it by the time she had staggered that far, were very small, and she had no idea what to do next if he had driven away with her purse.

When, sore-footed and breathless, she turned the corner into the street where the Lotus had been parked, David was sitting at the wheel, his shirtsleeved arm resting along the top of the open window. She crossed the road and drew level with the car. He didn't turn, but he must have been watching her in the wing mirror because he brought up his hand, holding her bag.

"Will you be needing this?"

"Thank you," Jenny muttered ungraciously, taking it from him and limping on. She passed the front of the car and crossed to the pavement on the passenger side, walking stiffly, conscious of his gaze following her movements. He started the engine, but the car only slid forward a few yards, passed her, and stopped again. The passenger door opened. David leaned across as she drew level.

"What happened to your shoe?"

"I broke a heel. Isn't that obvious?" she replied icily.

He gave a reluctant snort of laughter. "Too bad," he said. "It's very difficult to be on your dignity in bare feet, isn't it? Get in."

"No, thanks."

"Oh, for heaven's sake!" He lost his temper. "*Will* you get in, and stop sulking like a five-year-old! I've had just about enough for one day."

Jenny climbed into the car without a word. It was a relief to sit down. She stared stubbornly ahead of her, and David didn't say anything else. They drove into Paris in a stony silence which lasted until he parked in the quiet square outside the hotel, and waited, expressionless, for her to get out. Then

Jenny said in a small, tight voice, "I'm sorry. You're perfectly right. I have been behaving like a five-year-old."

He stared at her for a moment, still unfriendly, then he grinned, the warm, personal grin which lit up his eyes and made her heart jump.

"Forget it," he said. "It was my fault, too. It always is. Are we on speaking terms again?"

Jenny nodded. The tight knot of tension was rapidly diminishing and she made one of those sudden leaps from angry misery into blinding happiness which came so disturbingly often these days. "I'm not normally like this," she said. "I don't know what's the matter with me."

David's grin broadened. "Don't you?" he said. "I reckon I do." Then his voice changed. "Trouble is, I can't be sure."

"Well, if you ever are, explain it to me, will you?"

"I'll do just that one of these days."

8

JENNY had caught the sun. Her cheeks were flushed and her green eyes sparkled. When she took off her dress for a shower, the tanned area above her dress' neckline was sharply defined against the creamy colour of the skin below. She brushed her thick hair into order and caught herself smiling dreamily at her reflection in the mirror. 'This is crazy,' she pulled herself up sharply. 'So he was nice to you. What does that prove?' It didn't alter the fact of his involvement, whatever that was, with Angela Torrance, about which Marcel had dropped those disquieting hints. It didn't wipe out the way he kept rushing off to keep 'appointments,' either. Again, she remembered Marcel saying lightly, "You are in a bad mood, David. Didn't you have a good afternoon with Maxine?" in that manner which *just* insinuated...she wasn't sure what.

There was no way that she could turn a few isolated looks, a few phrases with more-than-ordinary warmth in them, into an indication that David Maine regarded her, Jenny, as anything other than a rather inconvenient duty to be fulfilled on behalf of an old friend. She would have to be very careful, she told herself, because to be strictly realistic about it, she was in danger of falling in love with David... to be more strictly realistic, she already had. The girl in the mirror looked back at her with anxious, uncertain eyes.

The room had been tidied, and the bed make by the chambermaid while she was out. Marcel's note was propped tidily against the bedside light, reminding her that she was supposed to ring him if she was unable to meet him for supper, as he had suggested. It hardly seemed fair to let Marcel take her out, feeling as she did about David. She dialled the number on the notepaper and the phone was answered by Dominic, the manservant. No, he said, Monsieur de Roseul was not there at present. He was not expected back until later this evening. Could he take a message?

"*Non, merci. Ce n'est pas rien,*" Jenny said. She supposed there was nothing for it but to keep the date, and if Marcel made any further attempts to kiss her, explain gently but firmly that she wasn't available.

Just after she put the phone back on its hook, it rang. It was David, calling from a phone kiosk.

"Hi. It's me again. I just had a thought. I can be through by about nine-thirty. If you don't mind hanging on, and then meeting me somewhere in the town, we could have a late supper."

"Oh, David, I'm sorry." She really was. "I would have loved to. But I'm supposed to be meeting Marcel for supper."

"That's OK," he said, after a moment. "Some other time then. Be seeing you." And rang off.

He sounded as if couldn't care less.

Jenny's switch-back emotions took another downward slide.

She sat in the square, leafing through a French newspaper which she had just bought from the stand by the Métro entrance to help pass the time until she was to meet Marcel. She was reading slowly, not understand everything, when a smudgy dark photo on the opposite page caught her eye. David's face, Angela's back and profile, just recognisable in the blur of the poor quality reproduction. Angela was clinging to David with her eyes closed and he was looking tenderly down at the top of her head, his arms wrapped protectively round her.

Jenny remembered the flashbulbs popping last night at Hank Henderson's party. Even her hesitant French was adequate to translate the caption:'An emotional moment at Hank Henderson's party last night. Angela Torrance, 44, star of films and known for her part as Melanie in the TV soap opera, Prairie, with her constant companion, the handsome Anglo-American, David Maine, 28. Angela is in the process of divorcing her husband . . . one does not have to look far to find the reason.'

She put the paper down, feeling sick. 'Constant companion' was a gossip column euphemism for lover.

"It's a terrible photo, isn't it? Angela was furious when she saw it." Marcel was standing behind her; she had been too absorbed in reading to notice his approach. She flushed in confusion but he seemed not to have noticed the effect the newspaper story had had on her. She stood up, and pushed the newspaper hastily into the litter bin which stood beside the bench.

"You are looking beautiful, *comme d'habitude*, Jenny. And did you have a good day?" Marcel asked, kissing her hand with a smile that brought all the attractive wrinkles around his eyes into play.

"Yes, thanks." Jenny smiled back. Despite her preoccupation with the thought of David, she could not remain immune to Marcel's effortless charm.

"For myself," he said, "I have had a terrible day. Angela has been in a mood. *Mon Dieu*, what a mood! Nothing is right for her. She has sacked Céline . . . and the entire staff is resigning too, in protest. Only Dominic is left, and that is only because he lives at the house and cannot walk out at a moment's notice like the others who live in the village."

"Oh dear," Jenny said. "What will happen now? What about Laurie?"

He shrugged. "In fact, it is not serious. The staff work for my father, not for Angela. She does not have the power to dismiss anyone. But I think it is time she is taught a lesson, so I do not tell her this. The servants will have a little holiday, and in a day or two I will smooth all the ruffled feathers, and *if* she apologises, she will have her staff back."

"But is anyone looking after Laurie? Now, I mean?"

"Angela is there. She can do it. It is time she took a little responsibility for her daughter." He changed the subject. "Anyway, after a day such as I have had, I am in need of as much care and consolation as you can give me. Are you very hungry? Is it necessary that we eat straight away?"

"No. Not if you have anything else in mind."

"I hoped you would say that," he said with satisfaction. "I have two tickets for a show in one of the small theatres — how do you call them? Fringe? — for a comedienne who is very well spoken of. The show begins at nine and lasts for one hour, so if you do not mind waiting for your supper . . . ?"

"No, of course I don't. It sounds great," Jenny said.

The comedienne was an outrageous Frenchwoman with a deep, expressive voice and an acting ability which was a development of mime. Jenny had not expected to follow much of the act, because rapidly-spoken French was beyond her comprehension, but the humour of the woman's act depended largely on her acute observation of the bodily gestures and facial contortions of ordinary people in ordinary situations.

She caricatured fat housewives trying to cheat during a weighing session, people in queues, people at the breakfast table ... and finished with a telephone conversation, playing both parts, in which a suspicious wife cross-questioned her husband about just why he was working late at the office, while the errant husband tried desperately to fend off her questions, meanwhile under constant assault from his insatiable girl friend, who was (invisibly) wrapped around him throughout his injured-innocent protestations. It would have been comprehensible and hilarious in any language, and Jenny laughed until her sides ached.

They came out into the lamplit street, relaxed and laughing. "And now," said Marcel, "we will go back to my apartment, and I will show you what a good cook I am."

"Oh," said Jenny, blankly, caught

offguard. Supper out in a restaurant with Marcel was one thing, but an intimate meal alone with him in his flat at Angela's was quite another. "I don't know . . . that is . . . " She couldn't think of a polite way to say that she didn't want to go home with him. He smoothly disposed of her objections.

"Oh, Jenny, you cannot disappoint me . . . I have spent a lot of time on cooking for you the most delicious meal I could think of. You can imagine my feelings if I have to throw it all away."

"Well . . . " Jenny said, doubtfully. "All right, then. But I mustn't be back too late." At least this time she had remembered to get a key from the hotel reception, just in case. But she would prefer Marcel not to know that. It would be an excuse to get back before midnight.

Marcel's flat was in a wing of the big house, at the back, and had its own private entrance. It had been converted from an old dairy, and even had a separate driveway leading to it, approached across farmland. The windows faced out towards the fields, and it was possible to imagine that it was entirely separate from the main house. "I had it arranged so," Marcel said. "I prefer that Angela, and the staff, do not always know everything that I do. If I am needed, they reach me by telephone. Otherwise, this is my private place."

He had not been exaggerating about his cooking. Like most men who bother to take an interest, he was expert. The table in his comfortable salon had been laid ready, with linen and silver and candles waiting to be lit, at the sight of which Jenny started to worry all over again. However, his manner was reassuringly light and courteous, as it had been in the past, and she felt a fool for harbouring such suspicions. Was she turning into one of those dreary girls who went round imagining that every man they met was lusting after them?

She ate the meal with enjoyment, a little marred by her apprehensions, but tried not to drink too much of the wine with which he kept trying to top up her glass. "Why not?" he asked, as she refused a third refilling. "It will help you to relax."

"I think I'm quite relaxed already, thank you."

"No, you are very tense," he said softly. "And you look uncomfortable. Aren't you too warm in that dress?" It was a silk shirt-waister, with long sleeves and a buttoned front, and she had buttoned it higher than she would normally have done, specifically to avoid giving Marcel any ideas about her availability.

"No, I'm perfectly all right," she said, not strictly truthfully. It was very warm, and the wine and the candles didn't help.

"For myself," he said, "I am extremely hot. What I would like now is a swim. How about you?"

"Now? In the dark?"

"Yes, now. Don't worry, it isn't dangerous. The pool is floodlit. I often swim in the night. It is very pleasant —

much more so than in the daytime, in fact. Try it."

It was not the dangers of swimming in the dark of which Jenny was most wary, but the idea of a floodlit pool on this warm night was most tempting. If only she could trust Marcel... He hadn't given her any cause for alarm so far this evening, but would he be as distant if she took off most of her clothes?

"I ought to be going back," she said, wavering. "But I suppose a quick swim would be all right."

"Good. Then I will take you back afterwards, if that is what you wish," he said. "Have you got the vital key?"

"Yes, here it is." She took it out of the pocket of her dress to show him, then replaced it again. It was almost midnight now anyway, so it was no use pretending that she would have to get back to the hotel before the door was locked.

They walked round the side of the building that held Marcel's apartment, using a torch to find their way. There was moonlight, but not enough to see clearly. The main house was in darkness, and rather eerily silent.

"It looks as if there's no one there at all," Jenny whispered. Then she saw a faint light in one of the second-floor rooms, just visible through a parting in the curtains.

"Whose room is that?" she asked.

"Laurie's. She has a nightlight," he said. "She has nightmares sometimes. Angela's room is next door. It is odd that she is not awake, usually she stays up very late, but perhaps she has taken some of her sleeping pills, after the day she has had."

As they reached the corner of the house nearest to the pool, Marcel reached inside a small metal box screwed to the wall and turned on a switch. Beyond the tall yew hedges, the floodlights in the pool garden came on. "There," said Marcel. He led the way to the Greek temple changing room and started to follow her inside.

"Oh. Are you coming too?" Jenny asked.

"Yes, of course," he said, surprised. "Why not?"

"I . . . I'm not used to changing in front of a man."

"Then you should get used to it," he said gently. He looked at her in the dim light which shone through the open doorway from the floodlights. "Funny Jenny," he murmured. "So shy and modest. But you are not all cool, are you, Jenny?" He put up his hand and stroked it against her cheek, expertly sensitive. "You're not frightened of me, are you?" he murmured.

"No, of course not." But she was trembling with nerves.

"You must not be frightened. I am not going to hurt you." He put his hands on her shoulders and drew her carefully towards him, again so gently that is was difficult to resist such a quiet, tactful beginning to an embrace. He started to kiss her, beginning with her hair, then the side of her face, moving round by degrees towards her mouth so slowly and yet inevitably that it began to feel like the natural thing to be doing . . . And it was pleasant to be kissed like this, in this expert way by a man who was so much the embodiment of a schoolgirl's dream: the older, experienced French lover, with his sensuous accent, with his good looks, his aristocratic birth and his come-to-bed eyes.

If only she had never met David, she might have given way to his mannerly, unthreatening seduction, learnt some kind of lesson of love-making from it, and gone away without regrets at the end — she had no illusions that she was of anything but a temporary interest to the worldly Marcel. But she had met David, and it was impossible, she realised, to kiss Marcel with another man's face imprinted so clearly on her mind.

She pushed him away. "Stop it, Marcel," she said unsteadily. "We've had a lovely evening so far, and I don't want to spoil it."

"Why should it be spoiled?" he asked. Not angrily but reasonably, as if to a stubborn child. "There is nothing bad about love, Jenny. It is fun. It can be beautiful, if it is well done. You cannot pretend that I repel you."

"No, you don't. Of course you don't. You're a tremendously attractive man."

"Well, then? Why don't we . . . ?" He closed in on her again, with more determination this time.

She backed away again. "Please, Marcel. Stop it. I want to go home now."

And suddenly he switched off the charm and became impatient, his voice roughening.

"That is enough, Jenny. Even English modesty can be a little wearing, when carried to excess. I think it is time that we stopped pretending that you are going back to your hotel tonight."

"I'm going," Jenny said. "And if you won't take me, I'll have to ring the bell at the house and borrow their phone."

"And how do you propose to get in, if and when you get back?" he asked silkily.

"With my key — oh!" She had groped

instinctively for her pocket, and almost before her hand reached it, she knew it was empty. He had removed the key while he was kissing her a few moments earlier. Now he held it up mockingly between his forefinger and thumb, before placing it firmly in his own pocket. "No, Jenny — " he began.

She took to her heels. It was a silly thing to do, she realised before she had gone more than a few yards, because he took it as part of a game she was playing, her hard-to-get game. He ran after her, laughing softly. He was fast and fit, her heels were unsuitable, the garden was dark and unfamiliar, and she hadn't a hope of escaping him. Almost as she realised this, her foot slipped into a half-seen flowerbed and she fell to the ground. Marcel was beside her in an instant.

"No," she protested, managing to struggle into a half-sitting position, and twisting her body sideways. She was lying level with the thick yew hedge which bordered the side of the pool nearest the house, and suddenly, through the gap at the bottom where the hedge was thinnest close to the roots, she saw something in the pool.

She screamed. Marcel's hand came across her mouth in a flash. "Shh, you little fool," he said.

She bit his hand. He snatched it away, cursing.

"In the pool," Jenny gasped. "There's something... someone... in the pool!"

For a moment, he disbelieved her. Then he bent his head and looked through the same gap in the hedge.

In a flash, he was up and running full pelt for the archway which led into the pool garden. Jenny scrambled to her feet and followed, her ridiculous high heels catching in the turf with every stride. They pounded into the paved area surrounding the pool, where the tall floodlights at the deep end cast long twin paths of light down the shining water.

At the far end, in the shadows of the Roman bay, half-concealed by the bronze nymph fountain, something was lying crumpled, half-submerged, against the coping. The only sound, beyond the laboured breathing of Jenny and Marcel, was the steady flapping of the hinged filter cover as the water lapped against it.

The thing at the edge of the pool was familiar. The bright geometrically patterened gown, the fair, luxuriant hair... Marcel started to run again.

Angela Torrance was lying half inside the shallows of the Roman bay, her luridly coloured skirts spreading across the tiled floor, shifting with the movements of the water. Her back arched over the coping, her hair fanned out on the paving stones, and her arms, dangling slackly at her sides, were bent into distorted shapes by the refraction effect of the light on the water. From her wrists, dark threads of colour seeped, blending and thinning out in the chlorinated liquid of the pool.

"*Mon Dieu*," Marcel said. "*Elle est mort.*" He stood there, staring stupidly.

Jenny splashed into the water in a moment, bending over the slack figure. Angela was alive, although her eyes were closed, and she was deeply unconscious. Her breathing was stertorously audible.

Jenny hooked her hands under Angela's armpits and managed to haul the inert body round so that she could support it from behind.

"Help me, Marcel," she called, gasping with the effort of trying to pull the soaked, limp body from the water. He moved forward uncertainly.

"What do you want me to do?" But he stepped into the pool, and between them they got the clumsy figure laid out on the grass.

"We must put on tourniquets," Jenny said, trying to think straight. Marcel was looking in horror at the dark stains on his hands, and on the trousers of his suit, where Angela's dripping arms had bumped a moment before.

"What is is?" he asked, in an odd voice.

"It's blood, you idiot. She's cut her

wrists. Give me your handkerchief."

Marcel made an odd, gasping sound and keeled over on to the grass where he lay as still as Angela.

"I don't believe this is happening to me," Jenny muttered to herself despairingly. She left Angela for a moment, and knelt beside Marcel. He had clearly fainted, and was out like a light. "That's all I needed," she said.

She groped in the breast pocket of his jacket for a handkerchief, but failed to find one. She thought of tearing of strips off his shirt to make a tourniquet, but abandoned it as impracticable while he was unconscious. It was too awkward trying to get at a sufficient handful of the material to be able to tear it. With a sigh of resignation, she attacked her own new silk dress. At least the material was thin, and tore easily, and the natural fabric should absorb bleeding more efficiently than an artificial fibre might have done.

When she had ripped off several strips, discarding any with mud or grass stains on them where she had fallen earlier, she tied them tightly above Angela's slashed wrists, mentally thanking heaven for the first-aid course which had been part of her schooling, years ago. Gradually the blood ceased to pulse from the ragged cuts. Angela was still breathing, though she looked deathly pale in the dim light from the distant floodlamps. Her deep unconsciousness, and her heavy breathing, suggested something more than merely weakness from loss of blood; she was either drunk, or doped, or both, Jenny realised grimly.

A tourniquet cannot be left on indefinitely, she knew, without doing lasting damage to the limbs. Angela must be got to a doctor as quickly as possible. Marcel was sitting shakily by now, still dazed. The house was in darkness except for the nightlight in Laurie's room. It would be hard to rouse anyone to help her, and she suddenly remembered that most of the servants were not actually at the house that night. If the doors were unlocked, she might be able to find the phone, but if they were locked, she would have to run on to Marcel's rooms at the back.

"Stay with Angela. I'm going for help," she told Marcel.

He looked blankly at her, his head resting on his drawn-up knees.

"What happened?" he said.

There was no time to explain. She ran unsteadily towards the house, stumbling in the dark once she got beyond the pool garden. As she came closer, she realised that a car was driving up the long avenue towards the house. Its headlamps travelled fast between the trees, and it swept round the corner into the gravel circle in front of the house, scattering stones and crunching to a halt just beside the courtyard archway.

Jenny ran into the light from the headlamps, waving frantically, and stopped, drawing heaving breaths, her eyes blinded by the lights. She put up her hand to shield them, and realised that the car was a silver grey Lotus, and that the driver was David Maine.

He got out hastily and ran towards her. "Jenny! What happened to you?" She must look a sight, she realised vaguely, in a ripped and half-buttoned dress, with the skirt stained with grass and blood. He was staring at her, horrified, and she heard him say, with sudden realisation, "Marcel! Has he been — ? Where is he?"

"No," she said urgently, trying to catch her breath. She had a stitch in her side, and her knees were trembling. "Not Marcel. It's Angela. Over there, by the pool." She gestured wildly. "She's hurt."

His eyes closed for a second. "Hell." he said, under his breath. "I *knew* it. She phoned me half-an-hour ago. She sounded hysterical, said she was going to kill herself. What has she done?"

"Cut her wrists," Jenny said. "And maybe taken some tablets or something as well. I don't know. She's been drinking, you can smell it on her breath."

He started loping towards the pool,

and she followed as quickly as she could manage; by now her legs were shaking and felt like cotton-wool. She supposed she must be getting a shock reaction to what had happened.

Marcel was still sitting on the ground, head between his knees, when they arrived. He looked up and gave David a white, sickly grin. "What happened to you?" David asked tersely.

"He fainted," Jenny explained. "It was the blood. I think."

"I feel sick," Marcel groaned. "Is she alive?"

David bent over Angela's sprawled figure and listened to her heartbeat. "Yes, she's still alive. Who put these tourniquets on? You, Jenny?"

"Yes. Are they all right?"

"They're fine. Good girl. How long ago?"

"Four or five minutes. If she phoned you from the house, half-an-hour ago, and then walked down here before . . . it can't have been too long before we found her."

David scooped Angela up with difficulty and stood upright, the dripping skirted legs and trailing arms drooping slackly against his dark suit. Angela's fair head bumped against his shoulder. "Can you come and open the car door?" he asked Jenny. "I'll have to take her to the American hospital at Neuilly. Can you check her room for any empty bottles, or bottles with drugs, make a note of anything on the labels then phone the hospital to say I'm bringing her in? The number should be in the telephone book in the house. Get Marcel to help you." He was already striding towards the car.

A Lotus Élite is not the ideal vehicle in which to transport an unconscious body, and it was with some difficulty that David got Angela loaded into the passenger seat and strapped into place so that she would not slip sideways across the controls. When it was done, he straightened up in relief.

"I'd better get going. You were marvellous," he said simply. "Can you do what I asked, about the pills?"

"If I can get in. I don't know if Angela would have locked a door after her. I suppose not."

"Here's a key, just in case." He detached one from his car keys and handed it over. "It opens the French doors in the courtyard."

So he had his own key to Angela's house? But there was no time to think about that. The car roared off, and Jenny was left alone.

Angela had left the courtyard door open, anyway. Marcel arrived as Jenny was going in. He was shaken and ashamed at having passed out at a critical moment. "I don't know what happened," he said. "You must think me a fool."

"You couldn't help it. Lots of people have the same problem," Jenny said.

"It is fortunate for Angela that you did not. Should I wake up Dominic?"

"I'm surprised he didn't hear the car."

"If he did, he will have assumed it was David. Sometimes Angela asks him to come over. He would not be surprised."

It was one more piece of evidence to suggest that David was Angela's lover. Jenny didn't want to hear any more. She had something more important to think about at this moment than the truth about David's relationship with Angela Torrance.

"Can you find me the number of the American Hospital at Neuilly? David told me to ring and say he was on his way, and also to tell them of any pills or drink she might have taken. I'll check her room now."

While he was looking up the number, Jenny ran upstairs to Angela's room. The place looked almost as if it had been burgled — Angela seemed to have had some kind of tantrum. There were papers everywhere: torn letters and magazines, pages of script, crumpled and scrawled over. Clothes had been tossed across the unmade bed and the floor. Cupboards and drawers were open. A photograph in a gold frame lay face down on the dressing-table, and when Jenny picked it up, the shattered glass fell from its face. It was a snapshot of a man, with a small girl, recognisable as Laurie, taken a few years ago when she was four or five. The man, fair and thick-set and good-looking with a square, good-humoured face, must be Angela's husband.

And there, on the dressing-table, was a small brown pharmacist's bottle, the label handwritten in French. It was empty. She could not make out the name of the drug. Beside the bed, an empty Beaujolais bottle stood among a litter of clothes and paper scraps on the floor.

"Jenny?" It was Laurie Torrance, sleepy and bewildered, standing in the doorway. "What are you doing here? I thought I heard voices. Was it David's car, driving away. This is my Mom's room." She looked around her at the mess. "Where is Mom?"

Jenny did her best to sound calm and unworried. "She's had an accident. David has taken her to hospital," she said gently.

"Oh." Laurie took it very calmly. "Is that why you've got blood on your dress? Is she hurt bad?"

"I don't know. But the hospital will take care of her, and David is looking after her."

"She's been crying all day, and shouting at everybody."

"What made her cry, Laurie?"

"She got a letter from Daddy's lawyers, about the divorce and all the settlements and everything. And me. She always gets upset about the lawyers' letters. There was another one yesterday . . . I wish my Daddy was here," she added suddenly, her eyes filling tears.

Jenny's throat constricted in sympathy. "Oh, Laurie, don't cry," she whispered. She knelt down and put her arms round the child's thin shaking body. "It'll be all right, you'll see, and you'll see your Daddy soon."

"Will I?" the girl said, wistfully. "Do you promise?"

"Yes," Jenny said. "I promise." If I have to go to California and drag him here by the scruff of the neck I will see to it, she swore to herself, that he doesn't leave this kid to fend for herself in this stupid adult mess.

"I have to phone the hospital now," she remembered. "Do you want to go back to bed, Laurie, or would you like to come with me?"

"I'd rather come with you."

"Well," she said, resolutely pushing her own fatigue away, "since we're all up in the middle of the night, how about a midnight feast? Well, a four o'clock-in-the-morning feast, anyway?"

"I'm starving," Laurie agreed, brightening up. "But I'm not allowed to help myself in the kitchen," she remembered, crestfallen.

"Yes, you are. Just this once." After all, Céline the cook had been dismissed that day, so there was no one to object. Leaving Marcel to contact the hospital with the information about Angela's chemist's bottle, Jenny raided the biscuit tin for Laurie, made her hot chocolate and then brewed coffee for Marcel, who had fallen asleep in an armchair by the time they carried it through to the study. Then they rooted through all the cupboards in the spotless modern kitchen and made chocolate chip cookies.

"Would you believe," Laurie said, happily absorbed, "that I've never even been in this kitchen? Usually the food just appears on trolleys in the dining-room under big silver covers. But I just love cooking. So does Mom, when we're at home." Her lip began to quiver, but luckily the auto alarm announced that the cookies were ready, and she was distracted by the business of taking them out and spreading them on racks to cool, and then tasting them. In the middle of all this, David walked in.

"Hi. What's going on? An all-night baking session?"

"Oh, David!" Laurie flung herself at him. "Is Mom OK?"

"Yes, Laurie. She's going to be all right. You can go and see her tomorrow."

"Do you mean today?"

"I guess I do," he acknowledged.

"What are you doing out of bed at this time of the morning?"

"I woke up," she said. "Jenny's been helping me to bake cookies."

"Do I get one?"

"Oh, sure." She handed him the plateful proudly, and he made suitably congratulatory comments. Then he added, "Don't you think you ought to go back to bed now?"

"Do I have to?" she pleaded. "I don't feel the least bit tired."

"Maybe not. But you will be tomorrow ... sorry, today. And if you want to go to see your Mom tomorrow, you'd better look bright-eyed and bushy-tailed or she'll be very cross with Jenny and me for letting you stay up so late."

"OK," she said resignedly. She wandered off upstairs, apparently completely reassured.

"I hope the cooking was OK, and no one will object," Jenny said. "She didn't seem likely to go back to sleep at the time, and it seemed a good way to keep her busy."

"It's fine. Great idea."

"Is Angela all right?"

"She will be. She's had a transfusion, and they've pumped her out and stitched her up and sedated her. She was conscious, drowsy and duly contrite when I left. She'll be thoroughly ashamed of herself when she wakes up properly."

"So she should be," Jenny said acidly. "Giving Laurie a scare like that."

"She didn't do it to scare Laurie," David replied reasonably.

"So far as I can see, she didn't consider her at all."

"That's probably true. You have to bear in mind that in the life they've led for the last couple of years, Laurie has always been someone else's responsibility. The governess', or Mike's. It's been part of Angie's problem that she had got out of the habit of regarding herself as necessary to Laurie's well-being. Or anyone else's. If she could see herself that way, it'd be a big help."

"But what's supposed to happen to Laurie while she's getting her psyche sorted out? Will her father take her over? I think someone should let him know what's happening."

"I agree with you," David said. "I was going to phone him, as a matter of fact. Or it might sound better coming from Marcel."

It might indeed, Jenny thought grimly.

"Where *is* Marcel?" David asked, as an afterthought.

"Asleep in the study, the last time I saw him."

"Well, it's time he made himself useful. Can you just make sure Laurie's in bed and all right?"

She looked into the little girl's room and found that Laurie had already flopped back into bed and was half asleep, clutching a giant teddy bear for consolation. She tiptoed out again, and was going back down the thickly carpeted stairs when she caught a glimpse of herself in a long gilded mirror which hung on the mezzanine landing halfway up. She looked terrible. Torn dress, crumpled and stained. Hair all over the place. Make-up smudged, and dark shadows under her eyes. She was trying to restore some semblance of order to her hairstyle when she heard the voices of Marcel and David, low and angry, coming from the corridor leading to the kitchen.

"I don't know why you make such a fuss. She had phoned you — she knew she would be found in time. It was not a genuine attempt, only a — what do you say? — attention-getting gesture," said Marcel.

"The point is, she made it," David replied. "Are you going to make that phone call or shall I?"

"It is the middle of the night," Marcel protested.

"Not in California. Anyway, why are you being so sour about it all? Because it's messed up your love life?"

Marcel did not reply, and then David added, "That's it, isn't it? You were doing the big seduction scene with Jenny?"

"Why not?" Marcel said lightly.

"Because she's got feeling, that's why not."

"Has she? Not for me, at any rate. Or I would not be involved, naturally . . . but she is ready for love, David. It is not good for a girl of twenty-three, a beautiful young woman like that, to be a virgin."

There was a short, intense silence. "How do you know that?" David asked at last.

Marcel chuckled softly. "How do you think? Seriously, David, that one is inhibited — now — but if awakened, there is the capacity for much passion. The man who helps her to cross the bridge will do her a service."

"One of these days, Marcel, I'm going to knock your aristocratic teeth down your throat."

Marcel laughed again. "Don't do it, David. I would sue you for everything you have. Seriously, if you are interested in Jenny, then there are better ways to relieve your feelings than by attacking me. And if you are not, then you should not be a dog in the manger. *Are* you interested?"

The answer, whatever it was, was spoken so low that Jenny, craning forward, failed to catch it. She took another step down the stairs and, to her dismay, the tread creaked loudly. A moment later Marcel came out into the hall, with a guilty expression on his face.

She said carefully and calmly, "Laurie's all right. She's asleep already."

She saw that he believed he had not been overheard. But David gave her an odd, sharp look, and said pointedly, "What about this phone call, Marcel?"

"All right. I'll go." He strolled away to the study.

"You ought to be in bed, too," David said to Jenny.

"I would, if I had any idea where to go."

"Marcel's apartment is through the kitchen, across that little yard, and turn left," David said. "Or there's a guest room along the landing past Laurie's room."

"Will anyone mind if I use the guest room?"

"Marcel might," he said drily.

"That's his problem. What about you? Where will you go?"

"I'll take over the chair Marcel just vacated. It's nearly dawn anyway." There was a faint grey light beginning to show at the edges of the curtains in the dimly-lit hall.

As she reached the foot of the stairs again, he said, "Jenny." She turned. "Thanks for what you did tonight. You were very good. You probably saved her life."

"It was nothing special," Jenny said. "Just the obvious, ordinary things." But the look in his eyes was warming.

She lay in bed in the ornate guest room, with an empire bed and a hard, unfamiliar bolster. Was it under the satin coverlet that David slept when he visited Angela Torrance? she wondered. Or did he share Angela's sumptuous king-sized bed? He had been concerned for Angela tonight, but hardly the desperate lover.

And had he been part of the reason for her behaviour, or was it entirely in reaction to some news about her divorce?

In the middle of trying to work it out, Jenny fell asleep.

Sometime around nine the next morning, Laurie bounced into the guest room, carrying a continental breakfast carefully arranged on a tray. "I made your breakfast," she announced proudly. "You went to bed with your clothes on," she added, surprised.

"That's right. I hadn't anything else with me."

"But that dress has got marks all down the skirt. I'll get you one of Mom's things," Laurie offered.

It was a relief to get out of the tattered remnants of her silk dress and shower, although Angela's vivid orange and purple caftan didn't exactly flatter her. She found when she went downstairs that David had already gone to the hospital. "And I will have to go myself later," Marcel informed her.

"What about Laurie?"

"She can go this afternoon. David said this morning is too soon for her to see Angela. She will still be heavily sedated. Me, I shall have to go to sort out the matter of paying for the treatment," he explained. "David said he will be able to drive Laurie there this afternoon at about two, and he hopes you will be prepared to look after her this morning, if I drive you back to Paris."

'Typical,' Jenny thought. 'Taking me for granted.' But she did not really object to taking the little girl out somewhere. "I read in *Pariscope* that there is a puppet theatre in the Champs-Elysées," she offered. "Will that be all right?"

"Yes, of course." He was not much concerned, so long as he was not encumbered with Laurie.

"What about getting her back here?"

"Can you take a taxi? That would be the simplest thing." He handed her some money. "I wish," he said, "that this had not happened."

"Don't we all?" Jenny said.

"Because it seems I will have to be occupied for a while — Monsieur Torrance is going to fly in from California, arriving later this afternoon, and I will be needed to meet him and sort out whatever needs to be done."

"I'm so glad he's coming." Her promise to Laurie would be kept, Jenny thought with relief.

"But you will not be here for many more days, will you? When can I see you again?" Marcel asked.

"I think it might be better," Jenny said carefully, "if we don't meet again, Marcel."

"Why not? Are you angry with me, because of last night? Something I did? Or said?"

"No," Jenny said, searching for some final, but kind way to explain that she really did not want to continue with their pointless relationship. After all, he meant well, and his interest in her, if ephemeral, was complimentary . . . even if he did think he was doing her a favour, helping her to 'cross the bridge.'

"The truth is," she said slowly, "that there is someone with whom I am in love, in England. So you see, I don't feel that it's right for me to go on meeting someone as attractive as you."

"In England? Ah, the fiancé. The one who jilted you?"

"How did you know about that?" she asked, startled.

"David told me a little about it, after the first day that we met. As a warning that I should be nice to you."

'Blast David!' she thought furiously. 'Telling tales about my love life to all and sundry. How dare he?'

"There have been times," Marcel said casually, "when I have wondered if there is a feeling between David and you? But you said not."

"No," Jenny said. "It's my fiancé, Piers, that I care about. I just can't forget about him, so soon after we . . ." She looked sad and soulful, and Marcel patted her shoulder sympathetically.

"Don't worry about it, *ma chère*. I

understand perfectly. Perhaps we shall meet again one day, when things are happier for you?"

"Perhaps," Jenny murmured. 'And that's that,' she thought, with relief.

Marcel drove Laurie and Jenny into Paris a little later, and said a formal goodbye, with a regretful kiss on Jenny's hand. She found that Laurie was a great help when it came to explaining her non-appearance at the hotel on the previous night. Not that Madame la patronne actually asked for an explanation, but there was a slight chill in her manner which dissolved when Laurie launched into a tangled account, in an execrable French accent, of what had happened. Laurie's French being very limited, the gist of it was simply that "*Mademoiselle Chatham a sauvée la vie de ma mère,*" together with a lot of mime which made the whole affair sound like a swimming accident.

They spent a lazy morning, first at the marionette show, then shopping in the Rue de Rivoli for souvenir presents for

Laurie's school friends in California and Jenny's mother in Kent. They followed this with a foray into the Louvre, to roomfuls of Egyptian mummies in which Laurie took a small child's macabre interest, and an unsuccessful hunt for the Mona Lisa. According to the many notices posted around the museum, '*La Gioconda*' was always just around the next corner, but they could never manage to discover exactly where. Then there wasn't time for a proper lunch, so they ate enormous '*Croques Monsieurs*,' hot dog sausages inside a French loaf which Laurie said she adored. Finally, they took a taxi back to the de Roseul mansion. There was no sign of Marcel, but David's car was in the drive. Laurie ran inside and Jenny hung around on the gravel with the taxi driver ostentatiously revving his engine until David emerged.

"Thank you, yet again, for looking after Laurie. Her father's arriving from California later on today. Things are a bit hectic here. I'll ring you when it's all calmed down a bit." 'I'll ring you' seemed to be one of his favourite phrases, she thought sadly, just as 'You don't have to' seemed to be one of hers.

It was the first time since she arrived in Paris that she had been left to her own devices. No one to talk to, or argue with. No one to meet for supper. Well, at least she should be able to get down to some of the work for George which was supposed to be the main reason for the trip. The trouble was that ever since David had started pointing out how basic the required information was, she had found it difficult to be enthusiastic about taking notes. She had a sneaking suspicion that he was right; it was merely an invention of her father's to get her to accept a holiday. She supposed that it was touching, really, to think that he might take such trouble on her behalf.

She walked around the *Conciergerie*. The vaulted stone rooms were chilly and sinister. There wasn't much to see — glass cases with revolution documents, letters and warrants for arrest; some dark, bare cells in which the French nobility had been locked up to await the guillotine. She wished that she had someone there with her to lift her gloomy mood with a joke and a warm, sardonic grin.

Walking down the Left Bank afterwards, past the book stalls and poster displays, she heard the snatches of the taped commentaries drifting across the water from the ferries. "Ladies and gentlemen, on your right you will see the *Palais de Justice* . . ."

It was at that point, she remembered, that the photographer had come swaying along the deck towards them, and David had put his arm carelessly around her, and afterwards as carelessly removed it. 'Oh, David,' she thought miserably. 'Did I keep missing my chances with you? Or was there never really any chance?'

How was it that in five short days a man could have taken such a hold on her emotions?

She had a lonely supper at a table on the pavement outside one of the restaurants near Trocadero. The waiters were pleasant, and chatted to her at intervals throughout her meal, which helped to dispel her awkwardness at eating alone. 'I'll have to get used to it,' she told herself. 'It's likely to happen quite a lot in future.'

In two more days, on Sunday, she would fly home to her flat, and the job centre, and the problems she had left behind. Even the weather was changing; there were angry grey clouds building up overhead. When she had eaten, she walked the mile or so back to the hotel, using David's *Plan de Paris* to find her way, window shopping to pass the time. She was back in her room by eight.

It rained heavily in the night, and in the morning, Jenny woke to a new view of Paris, grey and rainswept and forbidding. The cheerful market stalls in the alleyways were packed away, or camouflaged under a mass of black plastic awnings which dripped on the passers-by; the cars swished past with more than usual impatience, sending sprays of water flying as they rounded corners. Either the holiday mood of the Parisians depended on sunshine, or if it was still there, Jenny couldn't detect it. She pulled on her old, paint-spattered jeans and trainers, the scruffy shirt of Piers' in which she had arrived last Monday, and her ancient anorak, and went out to the Rue de Monceau, scene of Hank Henderson's party, to visit the *Muséee Nissom de Camondo*. 'If Hank Henderson could see me now,' she thought, catching a glimpse of her inelegant self in a shop window, 'he wouldn't give me the time of day, much less offer me a screen test.'

The museum was odd, and touching. It was off the tourist beaten track, with a rather depressed air about it. The few visitors tiptoed around the silent rooms, eyed closely by attendants who sat on chairs in corners, presumably to make sure that no one touched the exhibits. The house had been the property of a wealthy aristocratic art dealer of the early nineteen hundreds, who had carefully furnished it in the correct style for its period, the eighteenth century. Rich and beautiful furniture, rugs and ornaments, recreated the ambience of a town house of an earlier, elegant age. But the owner's son, the only heir to these lovely possessions, had been killed in the French flying corps during the first world war — and suddenly the reasons behind all this loving accumulation of beautiful things were swept away. The house was no longer lived in but turned into a museum, and the aviator's darkly handsome face, stiff in the manner of old photographs, stared out from silver frames in the rooms which were preserved as a shrine to him.

Jenny came out of the house feeling sad and haunted. She tried to imagine the chandeliers lit, the long, polished tables laid for dinner with the Sèvres service which had been locked away for more than half a century, or the Savonnerie and Aubusson carpets half-hidden by the dancing feet of the Comte de Camondo's aristocratic guests in the days when the house had been a home and not a museum. It seemed a shame to take away the life from such a house. But then, who could afford to live like that nowadays? Hank Henderson's friends, in his rented house a few doors down the street, would make short work of Sèvres china.

In one of the elegant rooms, with their air of waiting, she had seen a Louis Quinze armchair which reminded her of the one she had seen in Jules Severin's shop in Passy three days ago. The Nissom de Camondo chair, of course, was as refined and superior as the house in which it belonged, but there were echoes, in its crisp carving and comfortable curves, of the chair in Passy, and it revived the temptation to take a second look at Severin's shop.

She resisted it. She was out of work, and she had spent ridiculous sums of money on clothes since she came to Paris. At the price quoted, the chair was hardly a bargain. She took a bus to Nôtre Dame, where damp tourists in plastic cagouls lit votary candles in the dark interior and wiped the rain from their lenses to take polaroid snaps of that magical, soaring exterior which let in so little light. It disappointed Jenny that the cathedral was so plain, even depressing, inside. 'It's like Angela Torrance,' she thought sourly. 'All show outside and nothing inside ... though she must have something that I can't see, or why would a man like David bother with her? She may be glossy, but she isn't *that* beautiful.' Money, whispered the acrid voice of jealousy. She has money.

Late in the afternoon, Jenny threw caution to the winds and caught the Métro to Jasmin, and Jules Sevrin's shop. Jules remembered her. "You are the lady who came with David? Yes?"

"That's right. I've come for another look at the chair. Do you still have it?"

He did, but it had been moved. It was crowded into the main showroom, under a jumble of china and ornaments and mirrors in chipped gilt frames.

He carefully cleared a space and set it down. It was as beautiful as she had remembered, the glowing walnut wood warm against the torn cambric of the undercover, the acanthus leaves which wreathed the cabriole legs and arm rests minutely detailed in their carving. Exactly and satisfyingly like her other chair at home.

"It *is* lovely," Jenny said. Properly speaking, she ought to be finding fault as a preliminary to bargaining. The trouble was, the chair was utterly perfect. "How much is it again?" she affected to forget.

He eyed her acutely. "Four thousand, five hundred francs, Mademoiselle."

It was a lot. And she had no idea how to get it home. But she could hardly bear to turn her back on its graceful lines. "But since you are a friend of David," Jules inserted, smoothly, "I can sell it for a little less. The trade price is three thousand, five 'undred."

It was tempting. It was irresistible.

"All right," she said in a rush. "I'll take it." She paid him, and he wrote out a receipt, and then he said, "It is to go with the other things that David will collect?"

"Er . . . no. I'm not sure how I can get it home. Can you keep it for me until I've arranged something?" But it seemed that this would not be possible. "I am sorry," he said. "I have no room. I am expecting a new consignment tomorrow. It is for this reason that I made the reduction. If it is not to go at the same time as the others . . ."

"All right," she said hastily. "Put it in with them. I'm sure he won't mind."

She came out of the shop and the rain, which had briefly lifted, started to come down again heavily. It had drenched through her anorak in a few minutes and her hair, with no covering at all, was soon plastered to her head. The flowing waves of Raymond's creation, the result of a light permanent wave, disappeared into a welter of tangled wet curls. She put her head down and ran. There had to be a Métro entrance somewhere, but she must have taken the wrong turning on coming out of the shop because there was no sign of it.

Suddenly she cannoned into a figure in a raincoat, holding an umbrella. "Oh! *Pardon, Monsieur,*" she gasped. The umbrella lifted an inch or two, and she realised that under it was David Maine.

Even with rain pouring down his neck he managed to look stylish, she thought resentfully. His raincoat had to be a Burberry or something equally distinguished. As usual, it fitted perfectly. She, on the other hand, was a mess. She looked up, through a dripping fringe of hair, and realised that he was looking startled but pleased to see her.

"Hi. Jenny." After only one day away from it, it felt like a home coming to see his face again. A warm sensation went snaking down her spine at the sound of his voice. He shifted the umbrella a fraction so that it included her. "What are you doing out in this downpour?"

"I've been buying a chair," she said happily.

"Not that Louis quinze chair at Severin's?"

"That's the one."

He grimaced, but in a friendly way. "Damn. I was on my way to buy the darned thing myself. How much did he let you have it for?"

"Three thousand, five hundred francs," she said proudly.

"You were robbed," he said. "That might be a fair price if it was one of a pair, but for a single — "

"I don't want it to resell. I wanted it to keep. So that price is reasonable, in my opinion. Anyway, it *is* one of a pair. I have one exactly like it at home. That's why I particularly wanted it."

"How were you proposing to get it home, anyway?"

She looked awkward. "I was hoping to persuade you to take it with your things."

"After you'd pinched it from under my nose? Some nerve! OK, I can do that.

I've got all the paperwork and customs clearance down to a fine art these days. But are you feeling all right?"

"Yes, I think so. Why?"

"Because that must be the first time ever that you've asked me to do something for you. Up to now, it's been, 'No thank you, Mr. Maine, no need to, Mr. Maine, don't bother, Mr. Maine.'"

Jenny flushed. "Well, of course, if it's any trouble to you — " she began.

He touched a finger lightly to her lips. "Shh, don't spoil it. Let me savour the moment. Well, as there's not much point in going to buy a chair that isn't there, how about coming back to my flat to get dried out? It's just round the corner from here. You'd better have my coat,"

"But then you'll be soaked."

"OK, we'll share it."

"There's no point," Jenny said. "I'm drenched already."

He shrugged, and put the coat back on.

'Another chance missed,' Jenny thought. 'How do I do it?'

"On the other hand," she said, taking a deep breath, "if you're prepared to share, thanks." A moment later she was walking up the road with David's arm around her shoulders, and his coat pulled around the pair of them. He held the umbrella over their heads, and for practical purposes it was necessary that he held her close to him.

Jenny no longer minded Paris in the rain.

9

THE flat was in the Avenue Mozart, the main street which ran straight uphill to the Place de Passy and the La Muette Métro station. It was on the first floor of one of the elegant buildings, with their solid wrought-iron and glass swing doors, glimpses of marbled halls, stone pillars and sweeping stairways beyond, that gave the district the affectionate tag of 'Classy Passy'. David let them in and disposed of the two wet coats and dripping umbrella in one of the back rooms of the apartment, while Jenny stood in the doorway of the gracious drawing-room, feeling shy and extremely soggy.

The room was beautifully and expensively furnished in a mixture of antique and modern pieces which blended surprisingly well. She recognised a Louis Quinze writing table against the wall with

Meissen candlesticks on its glossy surface. The carpets were inches thick and the luxurious sofas looked Italian. David had said the flat was borrowed, along with the sleek Lotus car. Whoever the owner was, lack of cash was not one of his — or her — problems.

David came in from the bathroom. There were wet patches all over the front and sleeve of his shirt where it had come into contact with Jenny's soaked anorak, she noticed. He hadn't complained at the time.

"Oh, you did get wet," she said.

"That's OK. I won't shrink." He looked at her sodden clothes and hair. "You might, though, if you don't get out of those things. Use that bathroom through there. I think there's a dressing-gown of some sort on the back of the door."

There was. A lady's wrap in a soft, silky fabric, in a glowing turquoise embroidered over with vibrant oriental flowers. Whose? Did it belong to the owner of the flat, or was David just so well organised in his love life that he kept such things in reserve? She felt diffident about reappearing in a silk wrap and little else but, after all, if she didn't take off her wet clothes, she was liable to drip all over the soft furnishings. She took off everything except her panties, rubbed herself down with one of the thick, fluffy towels, then dried her hair until it was just damp and springy. She brushed it sketchily into some kind of order — there was no chance of recapturing the original style — and put on the turquoise robe.

As a means of cover, it wasn't very efficient, she discovered. But there was nothing else available, apart from her soaked jeans and shirt, and the thought of climbing back into those was repellent.

The bathroom was very tidy, but there was a row of louvre-fronted cupboards underneath the basin. She opened one and found shaving gear, talcum powder and assorted masculine impedimenta, presumably David's. Inside the next cupboard were perfumes, powders and cosmetics, in orderly rows... She shut the cupboard quickly, wishing she had not pried. At any rate, the owner of those boxes and jars was not here at the moment or David would hardly be making free with her dressing-gown.

She came back out of the drawing-room self-consciously. David was standing in the doorway of the lobby that led to the kitchen, shirtless, with a towel draped round his shoulders. He was using one end to towel his hair dry. Jenny stopped dead at the sight of him, wanting to look and yet shy of staring. It would sound incongruous, she thought, to describe a man as beautiful, but as far as masculine beauty was concerned, David had it. His figure in clothes had suggested athletic fitness. With the upper half of his body stripped, she could see clearly the spare, muscular lines of him: the well-set neck, broad shoulders tapering to narrow waist, the soft down of dark hair on his chest and forearms, and the smooth, tanned, resilient skin. His dark hair, curling a little with the damp like her own, was falling untidily over his forehead and looked even blacker than usual. She felt a shock of pure physical desire which left her shaking.

He looked up and saw her, and the blue gaze lingered. "That colour suits you," he said eventually.

"Thank you." She took a few nervous steps into the room and found herself by the writing table, staring blindly at the candlesticks. She focussed her attention on them, in a kind of panic, her pulse seeming to pound in her ears. "These are lovely," she said, her voice sounding strange and distant. "May I look?"

"Sure. If you don't drop them. They don't belong to me."

"I make a point of not dropping Meissen." She lifted one of the candlesticks carefully, examined the profusion of delicate floral moulding and the intricate tracery of colours, then turned it over to look at the mark. "Crossed swords and an asterisk . . . Marcolini period, around 1780?"

"You know your stuff," he said, with a note of surprised admiration. That nettled her — why should it be surprising? — and helped to restore her equilibrium a little, until he strolled across to stand beside her. Then her hands felt unsafe and she hastily put the candlestick down again.

"I made some coffee," he said. "Do you want some?"

It was in generously sized mugs, steaming hot, and she sipped it gratefully, feeling the warmth, inside her calming her nerves. She drank it standing up, chiefly because she didn't trust the silk robe to stay closed if she sank down on to one of the low, deeply cushioned sofas. "Did Angela's husband come?" she asked, trying to make conversation. Silences were too disturbing.

"Mike? Yes. He flew in as fast as he could. I haven't seen him, but I spoke to Laurie on the phone earlier this afternoon, and it sounds as though they've had some kind of a reconciliation. Apparently they're all going back to

California as soon as Angela is fit enough. So maybe the divorce is off, for the time being, anyway."

"Is that what she wanted?" Jenny asked, startled.

"Oh, yes. And Mike, too, I think. They've always been one of those up-and-down couples. She's miserable when she's not getting lots of work and media attention, and he's miserable when she is, that's basically their problem. But they're crazy about each other. I suppose they might work out a compromise eventually."

He didn't seem too upset at the prospect of his — lover? employer? — going away, back to her husband. "Won't Angela leaving make problems for your business with her?" she asked, wondering how to put it tactfully.

"No," he said. "I think I got everything I needed." Which was difficult to make sense of. She finished the coffee and stood with her hands curled round the mug, finding it absurdly impossible even to put it down. If she stooped to the low coffee table, the gown would most certainly fall open at the front as far as her waist. She could, of course, clutch in a modestly maidenly fashion at the lapels of the wretched garment with her spare hand. While she was deciding whether to look exposed or prudish, David came and stood in front of her, the towel still draped across his bare shoulders, and removed the mug gently from her hand. He set it down with a click on the polished glass-and-steel frame surface of the coffee table. "Well," he said, deliberately, "what shall we do now?"

Jenny dragged her gaze up to meet those sardonic, cornflower blue eyes. His level black brows were raised, quizzically, but she realised that there was a little pulse beating at the base of his throat, and that he was having to control his breathing.

He put out his left hand carefully, and placed it behind the nape of her neck, drawing her firmly towards him. Then his mouth searched for and found her parted lips. The kiss was all-invasive, like a torch that ignited all her senses, leaving her swamped and helpless, her mouth avid. The warm flesh and hard muscles of his shoulders seemed to burn under her hands. His towel was dislodged, and in time her robe followed it to the ground, almost unremarked in the fluid, dreamlike progression of kisses, response and counter-response, that carried her on a tide of sensual delight. There was nothing sardonic or deliberate about David now. He was as drowned as she was in the flood of desire, which spread, and grew, and merged until she found herself in a bedroom, with no very clear idea of how she had got there, and David lying beside her.

And at that moment, the front door to the flat distinctly opened and closed.

They froze. A light, feminine voice with a French accent called, "David . . . David? Are you there?"

He sat up, an expression of shock on his face. "Coming, Monique," he called, in a nearly normal voice. "I'm in here, but I'm not decent. Give me a couple of minutes, will you?"

"All right," the voice called back cheerfully. "I'll make some coffee. I am totally jet-lagged."

David turned to Jenny, his expression rueful. "I'm sorry," he said. "Believe me, I'm sorry. You'd better get dressed." And he left her alone in the bedroom.

She sat in the bed, her knees hunched, trying to collect her scattered wits. From the *salon* came the muted sound of voices, David's and that of the woman he had called Monique, who must be the owner, she supposed dazedly, of the flat and the Lotus and the turquoise silk wrap which was currently lying in the middle of one of her Italian sofas in the other room. At any moment, she might come into the bedroom.

What was Jenny supposed to do? Hide? Cower under the bedclothes and look guilty? Or emerge and brazen it out? David had told her to get dressed, but not whether or not to stay hidden.

She would be damned, she thought, with a sudden flash of fury, if she was going to lurk in the bedroom like something out of a Whitehall farce. Let David explain her away, it was his problem, and if he got evicted from his luxurious flat as a consequence of bedding a girl friend while the owner was away, it would serve him right.

She pulled on her still-wet clothes, gritting her teeth at the unpleasantly cold, clammy sensation. She dragged a brush through her hair, deliberately building on her anger to shut out the misery and humiliation of what had just happened. At the memory of those feverish, passionate kisses she felt hot with shame, though her body still tingled where his searching hands had moved over her. And in the middle of all that Rudolph Valentino stuff, she told herself, savagely, his girl friend comes home! Or should she say, *one* of his girl friends? How sordid!

Squaring her shoulders with angry resolution, she marched into the drawing-room. David and Monique were in the kitchen, talking quietly in French, while he set cups out on a tray and she poured sugar into a bowl. They looked comfortable and intimate together, Jenny thought bitterly, like old friends. Monique, an elegant brunette in her mid-thirties, didn't seem in the least put out by finding David in a compromising situation with a stranger in the middle of the afternoon. She smiled politely at Jenny and transferred a steaming pot of coffee to the tray.

"'Allo. Can I offer you some coffee?"

Suddenly Jenny's resolution deserted her. "I must go!" she stammered. Snatching up her bag and anorak from the peg in the lobby, she fled.

Running blindly down the stairs, hot tears stinging her eyes, she crashed into a man coming up. "*Pardon M'sieur*," she gasped, and stumbled on, leaving him staring open-mouthed after her.

In the street she looked desperately to left and right. She was about twenty yards from the iron railings, which marked out the entrance to the Jasmin Métro. As she reached the escalator which disappeared underground, she heard her voice called, urgently. Spinning round, she saw David running after her down the road, coatless under the thin drizzle of rain which had replaced the earlier downpours. "Jenny," he called again. "Hey, wait!"

She stepped on to the escalator, and was carried rapidly down into the tunnel which led to the trains. Ahead lay the barriers. She fumbled in her bag, groping for the *Billet de Tourisme* which David had bought her on her first Paris morning. She jerked it hastily out of the bag and a clutter of other things fell to the floor. Furiously she knelt, scooping them together and cramming them back into her bag. David appeared at the end of the short tunnel and ran towards her. She snatched up the bag and ran on, jamming the yellow tourist ticket into the automatic slot on the barrier with feverish haste. She felt an unthinking, urgent need to get away.

She pushed past the released metal bar and hurried down the stairs. David had been stopped by the barrier. He had no ticket and, coatless, no money. He was shouting something after her, but she shut her ears to it. With a distant clattering a train appeared and pulled towards the platform. When she glanced up as she stepped on to the train, David had disappeared.

It was two stops to La Muette. She sat on one of the little tip-up bucket seats by the door of the carriage and forced herself to take some kind of hold over her emotions. It was simply not possible to break down and sob in the Métro. She emerged at La Muette, and walked slowly along the top of the Avenue Mozart, through the Place de Passy, and then into the Rue de l'Annonciacion, the little paved alley of a street which joined the main shopping centre of the Passy district to the quieter residential streets beyond the Rue Raynouard. Her feet took one step after another automatically, but she felt exhausted, as if in a dream. The alley was almost empty — it was nearly seven o'clock, she realised.

As she reached the end she realised to her dismay that David was running up the steep hill of the Rue Raynouard towards her. He must have cut across through the back streets from the Avenue Mozart while she was in the Métro; and run fast, to get here so soon.

It seemed pointless to avoid him now. She did not feel capable of running any more anyway. She stood and watched him till he caught up with her, bending forward for a moment, gasping for breath.

He straightened up. "For heaven's sake, Jenny," he panted, still winded, "why did you have to go tearing off like that? You dropped your passport in the Métro tunnel."

"Thank you." It would have been disastrous to have lost it — she was flying home tomorrow — but she could not bring herself to thank him civilly. The words came out with a sarcastic twist to them. "I'm so grateful."

"What's the matter with you, anyway?"

"Nothing. I just didn't want to intrude on your little reunion with your friend Monique, that's all."

"Monique wouldn't have minded," he said, bewildered.

Jenny's anger flared up. "Wouldn't she? Are all your women so understanding? My goodness, you must have charm to keep them all happy — and generous — and you have stamina, too," she added viciously. "You're really something, aren't you, Mr. Maine — You even managed to fit in a short-stay tourist in an off-duty moment. Or was it an on-duty moment? Have I to thank my father for footing the bill for my touch of Paris romance as well?"

He had gone white. "What are you talking about?" he asked in a dangerously quiet voice.

Jenny was too furious to care. "Monique," she said, counting on her fingers. "Claudine, Maxine. Angela Torrance. We mustn't forget darling Angela, must we? And that dumb little

English girl, Jenny Chatham. Have I left anybody out?"

David's face was rigid with anger. "Just what do you mean? Are you implying I'm some kind of a gigolo?"

He had hold of her arm. Jenny threw back her head and faced him defiantly. "Well, aren't you?" she demanded.

He stared at her for a long, menacing moment. Then he almost threw her from him. "I don't understand any of this," he muttered, half to himself. "How could you think — ? What made you — ? If you thought *that*," he asked, with aching bewilderment, "how could you have been so ready and willing just now?"

"I don't know," Jenny said. Suddenly she was sick and tired . . . and confused. His anger and astonishment were genuine. She began to wonder if she had made some kind of terrible mistake. "Marcel said . . . " she whispered, and stopped.

"Oh, yeah?" He was instantly angry again. "So what did Marcel tell you about me?" He had taken her wrist, and now he shook her, not violently but with a controlled, white-hot anger. "Come on. I think I'm entitled to know exactly what he did say before I break his lousy neck for it."

"I suppose," Jenny realised, thinking aloud, "that he didn't actually *say* anything specific. He just sort of hinted."

"Oh, sure. That sounds like Marcel. And you were happy, weren't you, to pick up on any dirty little hints he might let fall? Marcel's problem," he added cruelly, "is that he thinks everyone's as unscrupulous as he is. He can't imagine I can be with a woman for an afternoon and do nothing except sell her a chair."

"So what did you sell Monique? Meissen candlesticks?"

"Maybe it's *your* neck I ought to be breaking," He said, slowly. At that moment, he looked capable of it. "Monique is my sister-in-law, for heaven's sake!"

"Your sister-in-law?" she repeated stupidly.

"That's right. You heard me real

good." Angry, his American accent and phrases were more noticeable. "And if you hadn't gone rushing out like something out of a cheap melodrama, you'd have met my brother Chris, newly back from the good ol' U.S. of A. As it is," he added bitingly, "you darn nearly knocked him down the stairs."

"I'm sorry," Jenny whispered.

"Let's take it step by step, shall we?" His cold, hard tone didn't waver. "Maxine: she owns five houses and two flats, and her husband's a top international engineer. One of her houses just happens to be in Oxford, and I'm furnishing it for her. We have the occasional consultation. Usually one, if not both, of her children is present. Claudie: now, Claudie owns a hotel in the classier part of Paris near the Place de l'Opéra. She likes to furnish her executive bedrooms with nineteenth-century military chests of drawers because she finds the brass corners are resistant to the stresses of executive bedroom orgies on the expense account. I sold her three I'd hunted out for her this trip, and she wants three more by Christmas. And, no, I do not demonstrate executive bedroom orgies to her. Where are we? Angela? Just what does that creep Marcel say about Angela?"

"He says you don't sell her antiques," Jenny said, feeling drained. His remorseless voice carried on, on the same dry and deadly note of fury.

"That's right. I don't sell her antiques. So shall I tell you, Jenny, just what I do for Angela?"

"No," Jenny said. "You don't have to tell me anything else. There's no need, is there? I've got it all wrong, and you've told me, and you're quite rightly angry about it. Now, please, can you stop shouting at me, because I think I'm going to be sick." He had not been shouting at all, she realised, but talking with a suppressed force which was as physically buffeting as if he had yelled and raved and hit her. She was totally exhausted and wanted only to creep into her bed in the hotel, and hide her aching head under cool sheets, and possible die.

He glared at her for a moment longer, then his face changed. "You don't look too good," he said in a different, gentler voice. "Look, I'd better get you back to the hotel, before you pass out or something."

She was feeling hot and cold and dizzy, and there was clammy perspiration on her forehead and her upper lip. David hooked his hand supportively under her elbow and walked her along the road to the square where the hotel door stood propped open like a haven. There was a familiar, raincoated figure standing in the doorway, looking out of it. She blinked incredulously, but the figure was real.

"Piers," she whispered.

"What?" David looked at her sharply.

"That man in the doorway. It's Piers Somerton."

A moment later he had seen her, and came striding across the square. "Jenny,

I've been waiting for you. I have to talk to you — I realise what a fool I was. Can you forgive me?"

"How did you know where to find me?" she asked, dazed.

"Oh, I wrung the information out of your father. Surly chap," said Piers. "I got this address off that wedding present parcel he sent. Anyway, the point is, I found you."

"You could have phoned or something. I'm going home tomorrow, anyway; couldn't you have waited?"

"Are you?" he asked blankly. "I didn't realise . . . Oh, well, never mind. The thing is, having made up my mind, I wanted to see you and say it and be done with. If I'd waited, I might have lost my nerve again. So here I am."

"You wanted to say it? Say what?" 'If anything else happens,' Jenny thought, fighting against hysteria, 'my head is going to explode.'

"I love you," Piers declared ringingly. "I want to go through with the wedding."

"Oh, Piers." Jenny closed her eyes. It

was entirely too much for one day.

Piers became aware, belatedly, that David was an unwelcome audience to his stated proposal. "Do we know each other?" he enquired politely.

"David Maine," said David, his hands in his pockets. He ignored Piers' tentatively out-thrust hand.

"Piers Somerton. I'm Jenny's fiancé."

"So I've gathered," David said.

"David's a friend of George's," Jenny said tiredly. "He's been showing me round Paris."

"Jolly good. Well, thanks a lot," Piers said possessively, with the consciousness of his two and a half years as Jenny's accredited boy friend in his voice David took his hands out of his pockets.

"Well, you've obviously got lots to talk about, so I'll leave you to it. I guess you won't be needing the escort service any more, Jenny. I'll see the chair gets delivered to your father. Can you pick it up from there?" She nodded numbly.

"Well, so long," he said bleakly. He hunched his shoulders and walked rapidly away downhill, through the fine, drizzling mist of a Paris evening.

Four days later, Jenny sat in her father's comfortable sitting-room and handed over the folder of notes, neatly typed and annotated, which had been the ostensible reason for her trip to Paris. She watched George glance through the pages briefly — too briefly — and put them to one side.

"That's marvellous," he said. "Thanks very much. Well, how was Paris?"

"Paris was marvellous, too. Naturally. You didn't really need any of that stuff, did you, Dad?"

He looked startled. "What makes you say that?"

"David. He said that you'd got all that information already. He reckoned you just strung a few questions together as an excuse to give me a holiday."

"Did he?" George scowled, the expression of a guilty man caught out in a deceit. "It's about time that young man learned some tact."

"But it's true, isn't it?"

"Yes," he admitted.

"Wasn't it possible to simply say, 'How would you like a holiday in Paris, Jenny?'"

"I don't know," he replied. "Maybe. But you're a bit touchy, you know. The few times I've offered you any kind of financial help, you've turned it down. It's quite a struggle to get you to accept a Christmas present. I just thought that if you'd lost a fiancé and a job in one fell swoop, a change of scene was sorely needed. If a bit of hole-in-the-corner subterfuge could get you to take it, all well and good."

"And where did David fit into the scent of things?"

George looked shifty. "He was part of the change of scene. I thought you two might get on rather well. I gather I wasn't entirely right on that score."

"Have you seen him since he got back?" Jenny asked, colouring. She had rung Monique's flat on the morning of her departure from Paris and had learned that David was already on his way home.

"Yes, I saw him yesterday, as a matter of fact. He brought me a chair."

"Oh," Jenny said dispiritedly. "Have you got it? I can probably take it back with me in the car."

"No, it's not here. I told him he'd better deliver it direct to you, and gave him your address. He wasn't very pleased with me," George recalled, reflectively. "What have you been doing to David, Jenny?"

"Why?" she said sharply. "What did he say?"

"He said, let's see now, his exact words were, 'Your daughter Jenny is a bad-tempered, aggravating, stubborn, screwed-up vixen, and I feel sorry for that poor Piers Somerton.'"

"Oh. did he say that?" Jenny said blankly.

"He did indeed. I gather he fell for you rather hard."

"Oh, Dad," said Jenny. and she put her head in her hands and cried.

Some time later, when she had worked her way through half the box of tissues that her father had sympathetically placed at her elbow, Jenny blew her nose vigorously and felt a little better. "So what about that chap Somerton?" George asked. "He came here asking for your whereabouts — said he'd tried your mother and she'd put him on to me, and that he simply had to get in touch with you immediately. Are you going to marry him, after all?"

"No," Jenny said. It had taken her about five minutes with Piers to realise, with absolute clarity, that she did not want to marry him.

He had stood in the square, totally unaware of the turmoil of her feelings as she watched David stride away. Then she began to hear what he was saying.

" ... You see, Jenny, we all carry a dream around inside us, I suppose; even sensible, down-to-earth types like you and me. And what I kept feeling was, well, this all a very practical arrangement but it's hardly the romantic heights, is it? And I got some silly notion that it wasn't too late, even for a staid character like me, to fall in love, real, head-over-heels in love, one day if I waited. But when I'd done it, called it off, that is, I missed you pretty badly. Missed having someone there to talk to, you know, and share things with, and not having to put on any kind of act. And I suddenly realised that asking you to marry me was one of the most sensible things I'd ever done, and changing my mind about it, the stupidest. So here I am, asking your forgiveness. We could still keep to the original church booking if we put our minds to it," he added, not waiting for her reply.

"No, thanks," Jenny had said. And when he stared at her, uncomprehending, "No, you were right. It wasn't the heights of passion. And it isn't too late for a real, genuine, knock-you-for-six, world-well-lost love affair. That's what I'm looking for, too."

It was some time before he was

convinced that she meant it.

Now she said to her father, "Piers and I are finished for good."

"I can't say I'm sorry," George said. "I have to admit I didn't like him much. Bit dull for a hothead like you, Jenny. To he honest, I can't think what you saw in him in the first place."

"I suppose I thought he'd settle me. Help me to calm down a bit," Jenny said slowly."

"Much better to find someone who's mad about you the way you are. Someone like David, for instance."

"Why did you ask him to meet me without telling him who I was?" she remembered.

"Because if I'd said, 'my daughter Jenny,' instead of 'Miss Chatham,' he'd have suspected me of trying to throw you two together, and he might have refused."

"But you *were* trying to throw us together. You are a wicked, scheming old matchmaker, father dear," Jenny said severely. "But I can't think what on earth made you feel it would be such a good idea for us to meet."

"Basically, because you are so similar. You do have a lot in common."

"Such as what? The antiques, I'll admit, but apart from that?"

"The other things you like. Books and music. Old houses. You both burn on short fuses, and yet you keep your deepest feelings hidden. And then again, there's the matter of you being at a loose end after Piers, and David having had the same sort of experience not so long ago."

She stared at him, incredulous. "You mean someone actually threw him over? I don't believe it."

"Oh, yes. Didn't he tell you? It was a very long-standing relationship, almost boy-and-girl next door stuff, dating from his university days. Not that I approve of these modern, 'marriage isn't important' relationships, but —

"Look who's talking," she interjected.

"All right. I'm divorced. I still think marriage is a great institution. So did

David's girl Sarah, apparently. She married some tennis player, out of the blue, and went to travel the circuit with him. I won't say he was heartbroken, because they weren't that intense a couple, but it certainly threw his life out of step. He's been a bit cautious about entanglements ever since, and it's been more than a year now. That's why I didn't say you were my daughter. I thought he might turn down anything that sounded too personal where women are involved. What are you smiling at?"

"What you just said. That he's cautious about women. I got the impression he was the Playboy of the Western World."

"*David?*" George raised his eyebrows. "Good lord, no. He's a bit on the shy side. Hides it well, though. So do you, don't you? Go on the attack when you're feeling nervous."

"But what about Angela Torrance? He certainly wasn't shy with her when I was around."

"Oh *that*," George said. "Well, that's

different. That's work. He's not above turning on the charm in the line of work. Otherwise he wouldn't be doing so well with the antiques. Anyway, I think he rather likes Angela. He feels sorry for her. Myself, from what I've seen of her, I think she's a perfect pain, and I wouldn't have the patience David does with her, coming out at all hours of the night with his tape recorder just to get hold of another epic dose of her show-bizz memories before they slip her butterfly mind . . . What's the matter?"

"I don't know what you're talking about," Jenny said.

"You mean he hasn't told you about the ghost autobiographies?" George said. "In that case, what did you think his business with Angela was?"

"I blush to tell you," Jenny said simply.

"Oh, lord. No wonder you had problems then. So you thought that he and Angela were having an *affaire de coeur*, did you? Well, well."

"Worse," Jenny said starkly. "I thought

he was a professional escort. One of those beautiful young men who gets paid to take lonely rich ladies out to parties and home to bed."

"Good lord!" George choked, and spluttered, and had to be hammered on the back. "And does he know that?"

"Oh, yes," Jenny said sadly. "I told him. He was . . . rather annoyed with me. That was the last time I saw him."

"And I take it you are now duly contrite?"

"Oh, yes," she said again.

George folded his arms and looked at her sternly. "I should think so, too," he said. "Well then. When do you propose to tell him so?"

"Down Kensington High Street," ran George's instructions. "Pick up the M4 at Brentford, straight through to Maidenhead. Turn right up the A423 and you can't miss it."

At just before six that evening, Jenny drove into Henley-on-Thames. The old town basked in the June sunlight, the daytime traffic filtering through and away. The buildings were a pleasant mixture, from Tudor, through Georgian to Victorian gothic, the effect achieved before town planning regularise the lines of high streets. It was just the sort of town she loved.

Jenny was in the mood to love everything about it. She felt pumped up and fizzing with energy and anticipation. She was going to see David. She was not going to wait primly at home for him to ring at her doorbell and deliver her chair, she was going to knock on his door and say, "David, I'm sorry and I love you, and will you ever forgive me for the idiotic things I said to you?"

Her father had supplied the address, and the impetus, for this bold act on her part. Her father was turning out to be a very nice man, she thought, driving down the road which followed the line of the river, in search of the small side street where she had been told she would find Maine Antiques.

George and she had had a more

direct conversation than any they had previously exchanged, and in the course of it she had managed to convey that what she would really have liked was for him to see her off at airports, not send his secretary, and he had shown her that the cheques and presents were not an attempt to buy her off but a hesitant expression of a very real affection on his part.

When he had said, of David Maine, "When do you propose to tell him?" she had stood up with a burst of determination and said, "Now. Or as soon as it takes to get to Henley." At which he had hugged her briefly and said, "That's my girl."

She was beginning to realise that she was.

There was the road she was looking for, and there was the Georgian house her father had described: detached, but only just, with a narrow alley on both sides separating it from its neighbours. She saw a gleam of sunlight on water at the end of an alley as she walked past it, having parked her car a little way down the road. The back of the building must look out over the river.

The whole of the ground floor front of the house consisted of the antique shop. The small-paned glass display windows that flanked the central door must have been original to the house, she calculated, judging by the narrow moulding of the frames dividing the glass. She liked the understated simplicity of the window displays, leading the eye back into the crowded interior. On a dais in one window a polished seventeeth-century chest, with a patina like satin, stood alone except for a Chinese *famille verte* bowl filled with pot-pourri. In the other window, a single Chippendale chair had been placed next to a pie-crust edged wine table with crisply carved feet which had been topped by a cluster of perfect eighteenth-century cordial glasses with airtwist stems.

The sign on the door said 'Closed.'

Disappointed, she looked into the shadowy interior of the showroom. It was only just after six now. She had hoped that David would still be in the shop but her father had told her that he lived in the flat above, for which there was an outside entrance. And, in fact, there was a small card, hand-written in David's bold sloping script, in the corner of the half-glazed door. "If we are closed, try the flat: at the back and through the garden."

She checked her appearance in the glass of the shop door. It would have to do. She had dressed tidily but without elaboration to visit her father in a pair of cream-coloured linen trousers and a brown cotton shirt, cut long and loose over the hips like a man's and belted tightly in at the waist with a broad leather belt. She was not wearing any jewellery, and her shoulder-length dark hair, with the auburn highlights glinting in the evening sunlight, swung loose around her face. She didn't look too dressed-up, she hoped, or too plain and unappealing either . . . She was beginning to feel nervous, and unconsciously crossed the fingers of her right hand behind her back as she walked down the alley towards the back of the house.

There was a narrow gateway in an old brick wall, and a brick-paved path leading towards the entrance door to the flat. There was a scent of honeysuckle pervading the small, pretty walled garden from a huge bush which had grown up and over the wall. The garden was full of old-fashioned hedge roses and Canterbury bells and riotous busy lizzies in a blaze of colour, and at the far end there was a big circular opening in the wall, framed in a sunburst of brick and gated with delicate wrought iron in a design like sprays of vine leaves. It was the type of gateway that is known as a moongate, and it gave a view of the river, with the sun sparkling on the water, which was breathtaking.

Jenny rang the bell beside the entrance, and heard its thin sound echo up the stairs which she could dimly see behind the reeded glass of the door. There was no answering sound from the flat. It occurred to her, belatedly, that he might not be at home. Or that he might be at home with a girl friend — George didn't necessarily know everything... Or that he might be at home, alone, and less than enchanted to see her. She rang again, her heart sinking at the lack of response from inside the building. She was turning away, feeling sick with anti-climax, when she heard a sound from beyond the glazed door and saw a figure running lightly down the stairs towards her.

He was certainly surprised to see her, that was evident; he stood in the doorway, staring.

"Hello," she said, smiling brightly.

"Oh, hi," he said blankly, his expression closed and wary. Her prepared speech fled from her mind, leaving her tongue-tied. He was wearing battered blue jeans, much worn and faded at the knees, and an old, open-necked denim shirt with the sleeves rolled up past his elbows; a far cry from the sartorial perfection of his Paris clothes, but it didn't make the slightest difference to his impact on her. He was still the most gorgeous man she had ever laid eyes on.

"I guess you've come for your chair."

"Yes," she said. "Dad said you'd brought it to him, and he asked you to deliver it to me, but that seemed a bit of a nerve after you'd brought it this far already, so I thought I'd better save you the trouble . . . " Her voice tailed away. If he heard the appeal in it, his distant manner gave no sign of it.

"You'd better come in," he said, after an interminable moment. She followed him up the stairs to the flat, feeling a rush of apprehension. This wasn't the starry-eyed encounter she had planned when she left George's Kensington house earlier in the afternoon. David didn't seem at all happy to see her. He was as remote and brusque as he had been at the airport on her first day in Paris. Either he was still resenting her stupid accusations in the Rue Raynouard four days ago, or her father had been totally mistaken about the way he interpreted David's feelings towards her. She supposed, with sick dismay, that this was highly likely. She had believed George because she so desperately wanted to.

David opened a white-painted door on the small landing at the head of the first flight of stairs and gestured into the room beyond.

"Do you mind waiting in there for a minute? I've just put a coat of paint stripper on to a carved door, and it's almost at the crucial stage. If I leave it too long, it'll soften the wood.

He disappeared through another doorway, beyond which she glimpsed a sizeable workroom crowded with all the tools and materials necessary to restore antiques. She would have like to watch what he was about to do with the paint stripper, but he had closed the door. So she had no choice but to obey his suggestion and walk into the room where he had asked her to wait.

It was a sitting-room, with typically satisfying Georgian proportions and fittings. The original moulded cornice and ceiling rose, and the carved wood surround to the fireplace, would have made it an attractive room whatever the style of the furnishings, but she liked the slightly faded warmth of the large Tabriz rug underfoot, its colours echoed in the cushions which were piled on the two long chesterfield sofas. There was a mahogany and cane *bergère* armchair by the fire, and various low tables carrying books and ornaments.

She wandered from the booksheves, where many of the books she saw were duplicates of her own, to the fireplace, with its carved mantel on which stood a small carriage clock with an unusual enamelled face decorated with a circlet of bluebirds nesting on interlaced branches. As she bent closer to examine it, she saw a photograph, stuck behind the clock, almost hidden. She lifted a corner, and found that it was the snapshot of her and David which had been taken on a *bateau mouche* on the Seine the previous week. She supposed it was a hopeful sign that he hadn't thrown it away... she heard his step outside on the landing, and guiltily pushed the photograph back into its place.

"Your chair's upstairs. Sorry to keep you waiting. I'll get it now."

"Can I come up too?"

"If you want to." He shrugged. "I hope you haven't been wanting it. I haven't had much time. I was going to drop it by some time next week, when I have to go over to Tenterden for something else." He could not have sounded more casual and disinterested. Jenny followed him silently upstairs to the attic floor, with its sloping ceiling and roof dormers. Half-open doors revealed a bedroom and bathroom, and one unconverted storeroom. Inside, standing clear of a jumble of assorted furniture awaiting attention, was her chair.

"Oh. You've recovered the seat for me!" she said.

"Only with a linen undercover. I didn't know what you had in mind for a top cover. Is that all right? I happened to be doing some others and thought I might as well do yours while I was at it."

"Thank you. That was good of you," she said gratefully. "How much do I owe you, for the transport and the cover?"

"It's on the house. Do you want a hand with loading it in the car?" She had picked the chair up by the arms, and found it much heavier than she remembered. "Here. I'll do it," he said.

As he took the chair away from her, Jenny saw his gaze resting on her bare, ringless hands. "How is Piers?" he asked, with his old, sardonic inflection.

"He seemed all right the last time I saw him."

"And when's the happy day?"

"There isn't going to be a happy day," Jenny said.

David put the chair down again with care, and turned to face her. "I thought," he said in an odd voice, "that Piers came over to Paris specially to sort things out between you?"

"Yes, he did."

"I gathered that he wanted to marry you after all."

"He did," Jenny said. "I didn't."

She held her breath, trying to keep the hammering of her heart under some kind of control. The look in his blue eyes was doing the usual powerful things to her stomach and limbs. She felt weak with love, and with the longing to be gathered up against that denim shirt. She was so acutely aware of the details of his face that they might have been etched on copper plate behind her eyes. There were still three feet of electric space between them, and the moment lengthened unbearably. Then she made the movement that brought her into his arms, and he was holding her so tightly that she could hardly breathe, but it didn't matter . She buried her face in his shoulder; the denim shirt smelled faintly of polish and turpentine and the clean sweat smell of a man who has been doing hard, physical work. "Oh, Jenny," he murmured into her hair, "I've missed you so badly."

"Me too," Jenny said. "Do you know

any cures for insomnia?"

"Just this one." His right hand tangled in the thick hair at the nape of her neck, holding her still as he began, hungrily, to kiss her cheeks and forehead and her quivering, closed eyelids. Jenny's arms slipped up and over his shoulders; catlike, she rubbed her cheek against his cheek and then, her inhibitions dissolving in the warm weak rush of desire, pressed her body against his body. At last he kissed her mouth, and the passion of it swamped her senses.

"How did you hurt your hand?" she asked, feverishly trapping his fingers as they moved past her face to tangle in her hair again.

"Oh, that." He looked sheepish. "Marcel's face looks much worse."

"Oh, David, you didn't fight him? It wasn't really his fault that I read dire things into what he said."

"It's OK. It wasn't really a fight. As a matter of fact, it was a bit of fiasco."

"What happened?"

"I punched him on the jaw, he bit his

lip, it started to bleed, and he passed out. So instead of knocking his block off, I had to trip round with the medicinal brandy."

"Oh, David!" Jenny collapsed into helpless laughter, and he joined in. "Anyway," he finished, "when he came round, he told me we'd both been wasting our time, because you'd confided in him that the real and lasting object of your affection was your Englishman."

"And you believed him? After getting so angry with me about swallowing the things he said?"

"I guess bad news always seems believable," David said, quietly. "I never could quite believe my luck, when it began to seem you might feel a little bit of the way I felt about you."

"And I'd been in love with you all the time. I think I fell for you the first minute, in the airport — physically, anyway. Then that evening, I started liking you as well," Jenny said.

"You didn't show it. Why not?"

"I suppose because I couldn't see

why a gorgeous man like you would be interested in a no-account scrap like me."

"Oh, I was interested all right. From the minute I turned round and saw you, in those tight jeans, with paint in your hair — and hopping mad into the bargain. I thought, 'What a knockout girl!' But then everything I said seemed to come out wrong, and you were so aggressive, I thought I'd blown my chances before I'd started."

"But I was such a scruff!" Jenny protested. "You can't have liked me then, I looked such a mess."

"Believe me, you looked terrific," David said. "You always do, as far as I'm concerned, even with rain dripping off your fringe... Marcel said you are 'gamine' and tried to turn you into a glamour girl instead but gamine's the way I like you."

"Poor old Marcel... did he bleed a lot? But it's your fault really, that I misunderstood. You could have mentioned that you were writing Angela's racy memoirs for her. Why be so secretive about it?"

"To tell you the truth, I find it a bit embarrassing. It's not great literature, is it? Strictly pulp stuff."

"George says you're very good at it."

"Does he? It was thanks to him that I started. I was just out of Cambridge, with an unspectacular degree, having spent too much time rowing and not enough reading the prescribed books, and I looked set for a career writing advertising jingles for cat food. I wanted to set up on my own with the antiques, but I needed capital to make it into the quality end of the market — it's a mug's game otherwise. I didn't want to scrounge from my father . . .

"And you wouldn't take a loan from George. I know. He told me. He said it was another of the ways we were alike, being stubborn about money."

"Well, I like to pay my own way in the world. George is very generous, but I like him too much as a friend to want to have him as a creditor. And antiques are a chancy business at times. Anyway, he went one better than a loan, by introducing me to a retired actor friend of his who was looking for someone to take care of the 'as told to' bit of his life story. I was puffed up as an amazingly talented young writer — which was totally untrue, I'd never done a thing beyond the usual academic stuff. But it worked out all right, chiefly because the guy had a great story to tell. So there I was, launched, if not to fame and fortune, at least to a reasonable income. Angela's my third subject and the publishers have another one in mind for me when I've finished."

"How will you finish, now that Angela's gone home to California?"

"If necessary, I'll fly over. I've got a good helper to mind the shop as I'm away a lot anyway, at auctions and so on. But, in fact, Angie's coming back with Mike to tie up the loose ends at Marcel's family estate, so I can do one last interview session with her then. That's in another week. Why don't you come with me? We could celebrate your birthday by doing all the corny things like going up the Eiffel Tower that I was too grouchy to do last time."

"How did you know it was my birthday next week?" Jenny asked.

"You dropped your passport, remember? So, will you come to Paris with me?"

"I'd love to," Jenny regretfully. "But I can't. I've got a job, starting from next Monday.

"Doing what?"

"Trainee negotiator in an estate agency."

"Is that what you want to do?"

"Not really," she said frankly. "But times are hard."

"There is an alternative," he said.

"So what is it?"

"You could marry me instead."

"Are you serious?"

"Sure I'm serious. If I wasn't, I'd probably have dressed it up better. I'm sorry it wasn't a very romantic proposal. What do you say?"

"But you've only known me for — "

"Ten days. I know," he said simply. "It's been a heck of a ten days." He tightened his arms around her.

"We've been fighting for most of it."

"I know. But as far as I was concerned, most of that was because of wanting this," he kissed her gently, "and not being sure if you did as well. Anyway," he added, "if you think we fight, you should see my Mom and her English husband, Bill. They're like cat and dog. But Mom says he makes her feel alive and, after him, everyone else just seems like a cardboard cut-out. That's the way I feel about you," he said, his voice almost unbearably tender. "You think I don't know you well enough? I know you. You're beautiful and bright and sharp and vulnerable. You're funny and sad and exasperating, and I'm crazy about you. I thought you could fill me in on the details as we go along."

"Oh, David." Her throat hurt, and she wanted to cry for pure happiness.

He said, on a less sure note, "But if

you think it's too soon, I can understand that. I didn't mean to rush you. I guess you probably think you don't know me too well... if you could just bear it in mind, I'll give you all the time you want to think it over. A month, a year, whatever it takes."

Jenny put up her hand and drew his head down to silence the diffident phrases with a long, surrendering kiss.

"There's no need," she whispered. "You don't have to give me time. If you're mad enough to want to marry me, I'd better take you up on it, before you change your mind."

Other titles in the Linford Romance Library:

A YOUNG MAN'S FANCY
Nancy Bell

Six people get together for reasons of their own, and the result is one of misunderstanding, suspicion and mounting tension.

THE WISDOM OF LOVE
Janey Blair

Barbie meets Louis and receives flattering proposals, but her reawakened affection for Jonah develops into an overwhelming passion.

MIRAGE IN THE MOONLIGHT
Mandy Brown

En route to an island to be secretary to a multi-millionaire, Heather's stubborn loyalty to her former flatmate plunges her into a grim hazard.

CRUSADING NURSE
Jane Converse

It was handsome Dr. Corbett who opened Nurse Susan Leighton's eyes and who set her off on a lonely crusade against some powerful enemies and a shattering struggle against the man she loved.

WILD ENCHANTMENT
Christina Green

Rowan's agreeable new boss had a dream of creating a famous perfume using her precious Silverstar, but Rowan's plans were very different.

DESERT ROMANCE
Irene Ord

Sally agrees to take her sister Pam's place as La Chartreuse the dancer, but she finds out there is more to it than dyeing her hair red and looking like her sister.

ROMANTIC LEGACY
Cora Mayne

As kennelmaid to the Armstrongs, Ann Brown, had no idea that she would become the central figure in a web of mystery and intrigue.

THE RELENTLESS TIDE
Jill Murray

Steve Palmer shared Nurse Marie Blane's love of the sea and small boats. Marie's other passion was her stepbrother. But when danger threatened who should she turn to — her stepbrother or the man who stirred emotions in her heart?

ROMANCE IN NORWAY
Cora Mayne

Nancy Crawford hopes that her visit to Norway will help her to start life again. She certainly finds many surprises there, including unexpected happiness.

TIME FOR LOVING
Kathleen Treves

When two young men are saved from their capsized boat and brought to Honeybank Farm House to recover, their arrival causes upheavals in the family, and Deborah has to cope with many problems until she finds time for loving!

THE SPOTTED PLUME
Yvonne Whittal

"I can only stand females in small doses," the arrogant Hunter Maynard told Jennifer. That was alright by Jennifer, her career as a nurse would come first in her life. Or would it?

SURGEON'S SECOND WIFE
Kay Winchester

A widower for some years, Senior Surgeon Nicholas Kent's life changes when he literally bumps into eighteen year old Venny.

ACCIDENT CALL
Elizabeth Harrison

When the Accident Unit at St. Mark's heard they were getting a new house surgeon they were delighted. But Tim Harrington was something of a playboy. It took a serious motorway accident to make Tim "grow up".

BITTER HOMECOMING
Jan MacLean

Kathleen had always loved Adam Deerfield as a brother, but it was not long before she realised that her sisterly feeling had changed into a woman's love.

LOVE BE WARY
Mary Raymond

The holiday of a lifetime with no complications. But of course she hadn't bargained for Ben Eliot and Eddie Ricquier, nor for the stormy emotions the two men would arouse in her.

ROMANCE AT REDWAYS
Jane Lester

Kenward Marr, the new RSO at Redways, could have told her that people don't always want to be "fixed", but Darbie had to learn everything the hard way.

NURSE DOYLE IN DANGER
Jill Murray

Heartache threatens Nurse Thelma Doyle when the ex-girlfriend of RSO Gavin Yeomans returns to the hospital as a very sick patient.

NURSE FOR THE SEASON
Pauline Ash

St. Chad's Hospital always took on extra nursing staff during the summer. But this year the intake was decidedly below par, thought Garth Ladbury. With one exception, Nurse Sally Anderson.